BASTIEN NIKOLAEV

A RUSSIAN MAFIA ROMANCE (NIKOLAEV
BRATVA BOOK 3)

NAOMI WEST

MAILING LIST

BOOKS BY NAOMI WEST

Nikolaev Bratva

Dmitry Nikolaev

Gavriil Nikolaev

Bastien Nikolaev

Sorokin Bratva

Ruined Prince

Ruined Bride

Box Sets

Devil's Outlaws: An MC Romance Box Set

Bad Boy Bikers Club: An MC Romance Box Set

The Dirty Dons Club: A Dark Mafia Romance Box Set

Dark Mafia Kingpins

Read in any order!

Andrei

Leon

Damian

Ciaran

Dirty Dons Club

Read in any order!

Sergei

Luca

Vito

Nikolai

Adrik

Bad Boy Biker's Club

Read in any order!

Dakota

Stryker

Kaeden

Ranger

Blade

Colt

Tank

Outlaw Biker Brotherhood

Read in any order!

Devil's Revenge

Devil's Ink

Devil's Heart

Devil's Vow

Devil's Sins

Devil's Scar

Other MC Standalones

Read in any order!

Maddox

Stripped

Jace

Grinder

BASTIEN NIKOLAEV

The Bratva came in the night and set the place on fire.

I thought it was my chance to finally escape this awful mob-owned club.

Goodness gracious, was I wrong.

Because the man pounding at the door is not a knight in shining armor, here to liberate this damsel in distress from her nightmare.

More like the polar freaking opposite.

Bastien Nikolaev, the new don of Miami's Nikolaev Bratva, is moody, broody, with a bad attitude-y.

And now, he's decided that I belong to him.

I'd call it the worst night of my life, but I'd be lying.

All the worst nights are yet to come.

BASTIEN NIKOLAEV is Book 3 in the Nikolaev Bratva trilogy. The story of the Nikolaev brothers begins in Book 1, DMITRY NIKOLAEV, and Book 2, GAVRIIL NIKOLAEV.

1

MELISSA

The illuminated sign over the door reads *El Palacio.* That never fails to make me snort.

If this is a palace, it's the shittiest one that humankind has ever dreamed up. And even though it's a new night, the shit is exactly the same as it always is.

As I walk out of the bathroom, I pause to talk myself into going through the motions. Even if there's not much choice.

But I can't help noticing it. All the sameness, like a blaring red flag emblazoned with the slogan, *What the hell are you still doing here?*

I mean, c'mon, here it all is, the past ten years of my life. The same mirrored, backlit-in-red walls in which I studiously avoid catching my reflection. The same black-and-blue paneled floor that I've had to mop down at the end of the day for a full-on decade.

It's not just what I see that's the same, either. It's what I taste, smell, hear, feel.

It's the overpowering smoke of cigar with a hint of the guava body butter José insists all the girls here use.

It's the endless repetition of the godawful Top 40 songs that José describes fondly as "money dumpers," in that they convince the patrons to part with their cash a little easier than usual.

I do another half-hearted scan of the room, even though I already know what I'm going to find. You guessed it—more of the same.

Eyes dopey with lust. Hands that wander, pinch, and grab things they shouldn't.

My face, on the other hand, never changes. I stick with *"All disgust, all the time."*

"A pretty girl shouldn't look so nasty," Tío Luis remarks as he approaches. His rheumy black eyes twinkle as he squeezes my cheek with one hand. His other hand gives my ass an affectionate pat.

I glide away from his touch, back into the club, while simultaneously offering up the best rendition of a smile I can. "And a bigshot like you shouldn't be wasting your time here, Tío."

Uncle, my ass. But I say it anyway. We all know the charade.

If it was up to me, I've had told these Cuban assholes to fuck off long ago. Left this stupid club, left Miami, left the whole damn state. Hell, if they'd offer it, I'd probably leave the planet.

But it isn't my choice where I go.

Because these men own me.

I'm so determined to put distance between me and handsy Tío Luis that I almost walk straight into Roberto.

"Well, well, well, if it isn't just who I wanted to see?" he croons, smiling with his shiny new veneers. He lost his old teeth in a recent bar fight.

I avoid his gaze. That tanned, square face of his might be handsome— if I didn't know what he was capable of.

"Melissa," he says, hand on my lower back, "meet Javier."

I turn my attention to the bald, squat little man at Roberto's side. "Señorita," he says, holding out a sweaty palm. A perfect gentleman—except for the fact that he's full-on gaping at my tits.

Then again, I am wearing the skimpy bright red sequined bra and skirt, as ordered. So I suppose it's having the desired effect.

No sooner have I reluctantly grasped his hand than is he slurping a wet kiss onto the tops of my knuckles, with enough tongue for me to wonder if he's mistaken them for the first course.

Don't freak out, I remind myself. *Behave.*

But I can't help pulling my fingers away with a tight smile that doesn't convince anyone.

"Careful," I tease the man, trying to smooth things over. "I need these."

"For what?" Roberto scoffs with flat eyes. "They don't help you dance —and they certainly don't help you sing."

Fuck you, I think. *They'll help me give you the middle finger, that's for sure.*

"Perhaps you want to take my legs, too, while you're at it?" I ask innocently with a *go-fuck-yourself* smile.

"Oh, heavens no!" Javier protests. His gaze slinks down to my legs. "That would be a terrible, terrible loss."

I shiver. The man's leering is making my skin crawl. He's like one of those over-the-top cartoons, with eyes bugging out, tongue lolling to the floor, and a big speech bubble above his head saying *Awoooooga!*

"Melissa will be up there tomorrow, you know," Roberto tells Javier, gesturing to the main stage, where Antonia is doing a half-hearted "dance."

She must have upped her nightly dosage of Vicodin, considering how slow her hips are moving. She's barely touched the pole in the past ten minutes. I've seen statues that have more life in them than her.

Then again, the only one who is really talented with the pole is my best friend, Kayla. She could go into the Strip Olympics with what I've seen her do up there. It's hard work, but it pays her well.

"I'll have to come back then," Javier oozes. He lets his eyes stray to Antonia for only a token glance before they return to me like an unwanted fly I'm not allowed to swat. "That must be a sight to see."

"I wouldn't know," I say with my most pleasant smile.

Then I turn and head for the bar. I really shouldn't, but God knows I'm not going to get through tonight if I'm not at least a bit buzzed.

"Your usual?" Manuel, the bartender, asks with a nod.

"And make it strong," I confirm. "If sex on the beach doesn't get me through tonight, nothing will."

He smiles in wordless commiseration. Manuel knows better than to say a single syllable against our dear employers. He's got more self-restraint than I do, apparently.

He's just sliding the colorful drink my way when more hands slide around my body. God, I get so sick of men and all the things they think they can touch.

"Hello, there, *bonita*."

"Hi." I extricate myself, heart pounding.

I recognize the man—Raul, one of José's guests. "That's not much of a hello," he replies with a frown.

He's shaped like a potato and boasts what may be the world's thinnest mustache, made up of a grand total of four greasy hairs, but Raul somehow still sees himself as God's gift to women. If so, God must hate the female species.

"Raul," I say in my nicest voice, "you know the rules."

I gesture to the sign on the mirror glass walls, the one José had to put up after Antonia practically got molested in the bathroom: **HANDS OFF THE DANCERS.**

Raul, though, doesn't so much as glance in that direction.

Instead, he takes another step closer, still smiling if you can even call it that. "Just like you know they don't apply to me. I don't need to remind you that José considers me one of his *closest* friends."

My heart drops. *Not again.*

Luckily for me, Raul travels a lot due to his shady business, so I don't have to deal with him all that often. Unluckily for me, the last few times he has stopped by, he's been pushing the boundaries of acceptable behavior more and more.

"Raul—"

"You think you're some hot shit, eh?" he sneers, advancing even further. "The Cubans' slut, their little marionette doll who dances and cleans at the snap of their fingers. You're lucky I even give you a passing glance."

We're almost chest-to-chest now—or at least, we would be if I didn't step back until the bar is digging into my hips.

God, he's so big and muscly, like a garbage bag full of ribeyes pinning me in. *Say something, Mel, say anything...*

"Raul," Tío Pedro says, coming up beside me. "Are you giving our Melissa a hard time?"

I exhale with relief. Pedro may be a hard-ass when it comes to how clean he expects the floors to be at the end of the night and how the stupid bathroom mirror can't have a single smudge, but he also doesn't stand for bullshit from our clientele.

Raul looks at me long and hard. "She seems to forget who she is."

"No," I hiss, hands fisted. "I absolutely do not."

But he's got somewhat of a point, even if he doesn't know it. Truth is, I don't know who I ever was, or who I ever might get the chance to be. When I was twelve, they took that away from me. Ten years later, it's becoming clear that I'll probably never know.

"I doubt that," Uncle Pedro is saying now. "She's just loyal. And I think we both know José wouldn't want you taking liberties with his girls. It sets a bad precedent."

Raul stands there for a long, long time, looking at me like a dog that's never been whipped before, until he swears under his breath and storms off.

I breathe a sigh of relief. *Thank God.*

"Thank you," I tell Pedro with a shaky smile. "I should've just told him—"

"Don't mention it," Pedro says, his caterpillar brows jumping high on his forehead. "When he has a few drinks in him, Raul can be a Class A *pendejo.*"

"We got your back, Mel!" another one of the Cuban older crew says from the lush red leather chairs they're crowded in. The others give me some supportive thumbs-up.

Something wavers in me. The "four oldies," as I call them, are as good as it gets as far as the Cubans are concerned. Sure, they're racist, noisy, and usually drunk, and when they've had a few too many, they make some cringe-inducing remarks about popping a Viagra and showing me a good time. But for the most part, they just harmlessly shoot the shit, tip well, and reminisce about the good ol' days.

In comparison to the other drunk louts who patronize this place, they're fucking angels.

"Tío Pedro," I say, "about that… Raul's been getting worse lately."

"Good thing I talked to him, then," he says with a stout nod that considers that the end of it.

"Yes, thank you for that." I bite my lip nervously, but I can't stop now. I've been wanting to do this, holding this in for too long. "It's just... I'm worried. That he might get to me when you or someone else isn't around."

"Don't be silly, Mel. Raul pushes it, but he wouldn't disrespect José like that."

"He could do it and then lie," I point out. "My word against his, no one would believe me—"

But Pedro is already shaking his bald head firmly, turning away. "Not a chance." A few steps away and he pauses to say, "You better get back to work."

I stand there for a few seconds, totally deflated.

Idiot. You big, dumb idiot.

Yeah, one of the old-timers may or may not step in to save me when one of our guests pushes things too far, but at the end of the day, I'm just merchandise. They own me, and they'll protect me... but only so far.

No one's going to look out for me but me.

I take another deep breath and try to blink back the frustrated tears. *You can take this. You have to take this. Do not let them break you.*

When I'm relatively composed, I turn around. Back at the bar, my drink is waiting for me.

I down it all in one gulp.

Then I slump there, waiting for my nerve to come back, telling myself the little story I've told myself for the past ten years: *Keep your head down, and keep looking.*

One day, they're going to slip.

One day, they're going to think I'm tamed.

One day, they'll let their guard down, and then…

And then what? Run and hope they don't find me?

Dye my hair, get some surgery until I'm unrecognizable and then, finally, finally, *finally*, have some semblance of a life that's at least mine, no matter how shitty?

Minimum wage jobs, shit apartments, no friends to speak of—all that is fine, all that I can handle, as long as it's on my own terms. As long as I'm free.

None of it is likely to happen anytime soon.

I gaze out at the club, then turn on my heel and head back to the back room. No point in standing around in the open and making myself feel even shittier. Yeah, I'm taking my break early, and yeah, someone will probably have something to say about it, but fuck it and fuck them.

I need this.

The back room is basically the size of two dusty closets and smells the same. Thankfully, it's empty. I sling myself into a half-broken chair, droop my head, and start to sing to myself. It's like a pacifier, singing. Takes me out of this nightmare and puts me somewhere soft and safe and warm.

It takes a few lines for me to realize what exactly I'm singing.

Ah, yes. I'm singing *that* song. Of course.

I don't remember its name and I don't care to, mostly because it belongs to that time I wish I didn't remember. *The Before Time*, as I call it in my head.

I don't like singing it—it brings back too many memories. But it's also the only thing that calms me down when my heart pounds and my skin crawls like this. So I don't have much of a choice.

It's the song Mama used to sing for me. I can still hear her voice, ringing in my mind.

Te regalo mi cintura...

Y mis labios para cuando quieras besar...

The song takes me away from here, this small musky room, this godawful hellhole, and brings me back *there*.

Deep in the warm, yellow-walled belly of our house, amidst the blues and reds of the furniture we hand-painted ourselves. Settling into the couch would kick up the ingrained scent of the roasted plantains Mama made every week, just because Papa and I loved them so much. She and he were as much of the house as it was of them: they wore the same bright colors, had the same warm aura, the same rich smell.

In my memory, the first twelve years of my life were just that on repeat. Safety. Home.

Then came the night that changed everything...

"Hey."

I turn white at the unexpected visitor and clamp my mouth shut. "Hey. Sorry, I was just..."

"Singing, I know," Antonia says flatly. Not because she's upset or anything. It's probably just those pills.

Even with the Vicodin slackening her features into a sluggish, uncaring mask, she's still beautiful. Deeply tanned skin, raven hair, almond-shaped eyes. The strong nose somehow only improves her beauty. Although she uses the guava oil once a shift, as prescribed by José, she always smells of the coconut oil she prefers to work into her hair. Her one act of defiance. We all have them. Hers is relatively tame.

Mine, on the other hand, are fantasies of violence.

In all other matters, she's a star. She dances when they say dance, looks the other way when their favored guests cop a feel.

She's even popped those pills as long as I can remember her being here. Five years now, if my math checks out.

They've offered me some of those innocuous, light blue little guys, too, though I've never partaken. Antonia is a walking advertisement of how much they make you not give a fuck, how well they blot out the pain.

But that's precisely the problem—I don't *want* to not give a fuck.

I don't want a trick, an easy escape out of all this. Not unless it's the real thing.

No, I prefer my pain, my suffering, my memories, thank you very much. They're all I have left. Of my parents, my life before, myself. If I let them take that from me, then what will remain? If I stop hoping that one day I can escape, then if I ever get the chance...?

Who are you kidding? It's been ten years and the Cubans haven't slipped up. Not once.

"Bad night?" Antonia says with that same lack of emotion.

"Maybe it's just because Kayla isn't here," I say.

I'm hoping she'll leave it at that. Antonia and I aren't on good or bad terms. It's hard to be much of anything when her emotional baseline remains stuck at a stubborn zero day in and day out.

"You two are peas in a pod," she says indifferently, cracking open a jar of coconut oil. As she scoops out a handful of the translucent white goop and starts rubbing it into her hair, she continues, "You should be careful, you know."

"I know," I say. "It was just that Raul…"

"I know."

When I glance over, I see a flicker of something that disappears in the dark brown of her irises. Some emotion. Some spark of life. It was so fast, so subtle, that I'm not sure I saw anything at all.

Then again, maybe the pills don't work as well as I thought they do.

"You just have to take it in stride," she continues as her oil-smeared hands run through her hair again and again and again. It's almost meditative, watching it. "Trust me."

"You're right," I say. "You're absolutely right."

"Then why not take the pills?"

"I want to live life on my own terms," I answer simply.

She shrugs. "Suit yourself."

Watching her, as she reaches into her purse to come up with a fresh fistful of Vicodin, it comes to me. "You're hooked on them, aren't you?"

She looks annoyed. "What does it matter?"

I let her question hang, because she's right. What *does* it matter? What does anything matter?

Ten years.

Ten. Years.

The two words are like a nail digging into my heel. I've been trapped here for *ten years*. And I'm set to be trapped here ten more, and ten more, and ten more after that. Until I'm too old to be any good as a dancer and they just keep me around to mop up after their messier jobs, like the nameless, hunchbacked old woman with the hangdog eyes I see every so often.

"Back out I go."

I look up to see Antonia striding out without waiting for a goodbye. She never takes more than five minutes for her break. The model dancer to a T. The perfect little pet.

I'm half-up myself, when a bone-crawling sound stops me in my tracks.

A scream.

Then a crash like the sky tearing itself in two.

Jesus fucking Christ. It sounds like every chair we have out there is being thrown, while there's a *pop-pop-pop* sound I know too well.

Bullets.

Someone's here and that someone came to kill.

I dive under the makeup table as the gunfire doubles, triples. I don't know how long I cower under there, trapped in a wordless terror. Too scared to move. Too scared to even hardly think.

If I stay frozen like this, hardly even breathing, maybe, just maybe, they won't notice, and I can escape…

I look out. Through the crack in the door, I can see the hallway that leads to the outside world. The red EXIT sign gleams in the darkness like a beacon.

I could do it.

Don't do it.

I could run.

Don't you dare.

This is it.

This is death.

I'm on my feet and starting to run when I freeze. Because a new sound has punctured the chaos.

Footsteps.

And here I am, caught in no man's land between my hiding place and my one chance to escape this nightmare of a life.

As usual, it's too little, too late. The door slams open. I clamp my hand over my mouth, but not in time to stop a scream from slipping out.

Not that I can help it. The massive, hulking man in the door is as pretty as death and just as lethal.

And his gun is aimed right at me.

2

BASTIEN

EARLIER THAT AFTERNOON

"The fuckers," Lukyan hisses.

Leaning back in the bullet-ridden armchair that stinks of someone's blood, I put my feet up on a face-down Cuban corpse. I've already done the rounds on the first floor and seen what they've done to our people.

The Bratva got in a few good shots, killed a few of the Cuban *pridurki*. But not enough. And we suffered some losses of our own.

The corpse shifts beneath my feet. Hm. Perhaps not a corpse after all.

I give it a kick, and the bloodied lump groans. Might as well start the interrogation with this sorry fuck, then.

"Tell me what happened," I growl at it.

Lukyan and Evgeniy stalk towards us. Lukyan readies his kick, but I stop him with a quick shake of the head.

Another kick would likely finish off this guy. Not that he's going to last much longer, anyway.

"We… came," the almost-dead man gurgles. "Lots of us. Twenty, at least… Big operation. José's orders. Took 'em out. Not… expecting it."

He dissolves into either laughing or coughing, I can't quite tell. Or maybe it's groaning. Or just dying.

"Why?" I say.

He gives a switch of his shoulders that might, in other circumstances, be considered a shrug. "Finishing up. *Lo siento y adiós*, José said. *Get it done and get it…*" More unintelligible noises. "…While they're down…"

I nod. I understand enough to get the point.

It's good strategy. José might be rash when it comes to bar fights from what I've been told, but when it comes to warfare like this, his instincts are on point. That makes my job here in Miami significantly more of a headache.

"What's he planning next?" I ask.

Silence, followed by a gurgling that could mean anything.

I doubt that it's anything I want to hear, though. Only a fool would reveal his leader's plans when he's minutes away from death anyway.

"I can end it, you know," I say simply. "The pain. I can end it fast."

This seems to rouse the poor bastard a bit. Bloodied and blackened face still pressed into the ornate tile floor, he manages to roll to the side and fix me with one half-opened eye. "…wipe you off the face of the…"

He exhales a long, ragged breath. Then the eye goes glassy.

Dead.

Fuck.

"This fucking *zasranec*," Lukyan mutters, stalking forward to kick the man.

I don't stop him this time. There's no point now.

Lukyan gives him one more kick for good measure, then storms away, thumbing his gun, head roving around in search of some other Cuban fuck to take his anger out on. Preferably a living one, I'm sure.

As for me, I sit back in the chair. I'll wait for my cousin to blow off steam before we decide what we'll do about this.

"They'll pay for this," he announces. His stout chest is puffed out with furious pride and his icy blue eyes are narrowed into slits. I pity the next Cuban who crosses Lukyan's path.

"They will," I agree.

I don't need to look around to know what he's seeing: destruction, complete and utter. A fucking graveyard.

A pretty one, though. At least, it used to be.

Bloodstained tatters of rich, rose-gold tapestries and curtains hang over the walls and windows of what was once a restaurant, billowing with a breeze from the smashed panes. There isn't one table left on its feet.

Someone dying groans. I glance around at the bodies strewn across the floor. There have to be about thirty dead people in here, at the very least.

Opposite me, Evgeniy is leaning on the remainder of a railing, looking almost jealous of the dead. The ones who are past having to worry about this, having to pick up the pieces.

As for us? We're a long way from the end of this bloodbath.

My hands caress my gun. I'm still restless. It takes me a long time to settle down after a fight.

"We were so close," Lukyan mutters sadly.

He's right. The past few days, he and Evgeniy had showed me around, introduced me to many of the major Russian players in Miami. Hell, I'd dined at this very fucking restaurant a few nights ago. I can see the table I sat at in the far corner. It's tilted on its side and surrounded by a handful of dead bodies still bleeding from half a dozen bullet holes each.

When we got the call, we raced here, but the question remained whether we'd arrive in time to fight.

But I knew the answer already. Even as I ran up to the smoking building, I knew. Because I heard it: absolute dead silence.

Miami is noisy at all hours. Even with the windows up, you can hear things. The noise, the bustle, the clubbers and partiers and the crash of the Atlantic.

But here, a normally busy street?

Not a fucking peep.

The only sound was the slap of our shoes on the pavement. Even the crazy hobos knew better than to stick around.

One step through the gilded doors and one look around in the gloom of the half-smashed chandeliers confirmed it—we were too late.

Until today, The Golden Bear served as a watering hole to a veritable who's-who of powerful Russian players and allies. It still does—sort of. But now, all of them are riddled with holes and gushing blood. Not so lively or powerful anymore.

As far as I can see, no one escaped.

"Jesus, how did everything get so much worse in one week?" Evgeniy sighs, as much as to the air as to us.

He's not wrong. When my cousins sent for me a few weeks ago, my father's childhood friend, Maksim Limonov, had just been slaughtered in his own home with a brutal message: a Cuban cigar in his mouth that left no doubt as to who was responsible.

And now this? Killing our people? Destroying our club?

The Cubans are driving the message home even deeper. They think Miami is theirs.

I'm here to show them just how fucking wrong they are.

"Maybe this is a sign." It's Evgeniy speaking again, his gruff bass voice and hulking form, as always, a contrast to his soft-spoken tone. "Maybe things are already too far g—"

"Shut up," Lukyan snaps.

He's still pacing, still restlessly playing with the gun in his hands. Growling, he spins and unloads a few slugs into a wall, then wheels back around.

"We didn't invite Bastien here to help us run away like little bitches," he finishes.

That's Lukyan for you. Abrupt and to the point. Clearly, us not having got here in time is killing him. In a figurative sense, at least. In a literal sense, it might've saved his life.

Because there's no doubt in my mind what my cousin would've done if we'd arrived in the thick of it: jumped right into the fray, spreading death to the Cubans at the cost of risking it himself.

I remember first meeting him. I was a child—eight years old to his seven. Father took my brothers, Dmitry and Gavriil, and me on a trip to Miami. Lukyan, even then, was bright-eyed and reckless. He snuck us out of his family's home one night and showed us how to jump across the rooftops. When the security guards of the buildings began chasing us, he just laughed and ran faster.

Evgeniy, on the other hand, the little quiet boy who liked nothing more than feeding his rabbit and lazing by whatever body of water he could get near? I was surprised to find him still in the Bratva business when I arrived here.

But I suspect that the man is hiding reservoirs of violence beneath that gentle exterior. His eyes show glimpses of it in odd moments.

"Tell me about José Correa," I say quietly.

"José Correa is a sneak, a fucking little shit," Lukyan spits immediately.

"Tell me something that's actually *useful* about José Correa," I correct with a roll of my eyes.

"Our fathers used to be friends," Evgeniy explains. "They worked together. Their own fathers were sworn enemies and sometimes, their men would have these little fights, but they tried to bury the hatchet, as much as you could with that much history."

Lukyan clears his throat and jumps in. "Once old Ivan died a few months back, it didn't take long for José to undo everything. Claimed our father had been screwing his old man out of profits. Started gunning down Russians minding their own fucking business. It's murder, plain and simple. Papa saw where it was going—that's why he reached out to you. It was too late, though. He didn't think José would go so far as to actually kill him."

"He underestimated the son of a bitch," Evgeniy says quietly.

"A mistake we have no plans to repeat," Lukyan adds. "José is unhinged, but he knows his shit."

"And?" I say.

"Let's see, what else?" He strokes his chin and ponders. "The man goes boxing every other day, they say. Rumor has it he killed his brother for falling for the same girl as him. He likes to oversee just about everything he has time for. Micromanaging little fuck. Used to be a fat bookworm until his father got him into the ring. No one really liked him except his old man, from what I hear."

"Do we have anyone on the inside?" I ask.

Lukyan shakes his head. "José has had everyone shot if he suspected them even slightly. He's a paranoid son of a bitch. Not afraid of the trigger, that's for damn sure. But if he thinks he can run us out of our fucking city…"

"Luk," Evgeniy prods. "Maybe we should consider—"

"Don't even fucking think about it," Lukyan snarls. "Don't even say the words out loud."

Evgeniy sighs. "I'm not saying we run. I'm just pointing out, Dmitry and Gavriil have solidified their empires in New York and Boston. Maybe, it would be a good idea to—"

"No," Lukyan says, suddenly weary now. He plops down into a half-broken chair that protests his weight. "We leave now and we leave Miami for good. We lose everything. There won't be any coming back after that."

Lukyan is right, of course, but I let my cousins duke it out a bit longer. I've never been one for wasting words. And Evgeniy still has more to get out.

"We don't have to run," he repeats. "We could broker for peace. The Cubans know we're serious and capable. If we just—"

Lukyan's long, high laugh quiets him. "You don't get it, do you, *sobrat*? The Cubans have just taken out our father, our leader. Now, they've come for one of our major bases. If we try to broker for peace now, do you know what message that sends? *Weakness*."

He spits the final word like it tastes foul on his tongue. I know how he feels. If there's one thing Bratva men despise in this world, it's weakness.

Evgeniy is more careful than his brother, though. Whereas Lukyan wouldn't think twice before charging headlong into a firefight, Evgeniy picks his battles.

There is a time and place for diplomacy and a time and place for violence. I'm still deciding which is more appropriate right now.

I need to decide soon, though. Without me, the Limonov brothers are liable to tear each other's throats out. They're too different, too diametrically opposed. They need someone to guide them.

Someone like me.

"It sends the message that we're ripe for killing," Lukyan continues in a low rumble. "You can be damn sure that that's a chance the Cubans won't miss. You heard what I said about José. Hell, you know it yourself. He doesn't just want a little more of Miami. He wants *all of it*. He wants to take our empire, kill our men, spend our money, fuck our women." He glares at Evgeniy hard. "You want to let him do that? You want to let him make our city his bitch?"

With every word, Evgeniy's head sinks further, until he finally mumbles, "No."

This should be enough.

It isn't, though. Because this argument has been building for years. Since the day they were born, if I had to guess.

"No, tell me, *big brother*," Lukyan sneers viciously, "should we just kiss goodbye to all this? Let them take our family home while they're at it? Leave the rest of our men for dead? Abandon everything our father worked for, make his life's work meaningless? Is that what we should do?"

"That's not what I—"

"Shut the fuck up," Lukyan says coolly. He stalks over to Evgeniy. "You've never respected what Papa works for. What every man in the Bratva has spent a lifetime working for."

"Just because I don't understand your—"

"What's there to understand?" Lukyan demands. "As long as we've been in Miami, the Cubans have tried to steal everything we've ever had. And for that long, they've used just about any means possible. Murder, rape, arson, theft. Our father's life was spent building a buffer that even those slimy fucking Cubans couldn't breach. To save us. To protect us. To protect the Bratva."

Evgeniy lifts his chin stubbornly. "Just because that's how things were doesn't mean that's how they have to be. We don't have to spend our entire lives fighting just because that's how we've been taught."

"So our father's death means nothing to you? You don't care to avenge it?"

"That's not what I—"

"He tried to play nice with the Cubans," Lukyan recaps for Evgeniy, though they both know the story by heart at this point. "He paid the ultimate price. He wasn't weak and he wasn't foolish. He trusted them, and it cost him his life."

"So what?" Evgeniy's voice is laced with derision. "Never trust anyone —is that the answer? Keep fighting your whole life, with your head always turned over your shoulder?"

"If that's what it takes," Lukyan says quietly. He pivots away, arms crossed. "It's not about never trusting anyone, anyway. It's about not trusting your enemies."

Evgeniy stays quiet. Either because he doesn't have an argument or is all argued-out.

After another minute or so has passed, I ask, "You two finished?"

Lukyan and Evgeniy side-eye each other. Evgeniy nods first, then Lukyan.

"You're right," I tell Lukyan. "We can't leave now. We're just getting started."

Lukyan smirks, rounding on Evgeniy. "Guess you're outvoted, little brother."

"But you're also wrong," I add before he can get too smug. Lukyan glances back at me in alarm. "Because running in and breaking shit doesn't solve a goddamn thing. No amount of Cuban blood will compensate for the loss of your father. Only honoring his legacy will do that."

They both look at me uncertainly. I rise to my feet and meet their gazes at eye level.

"Where can we hit the Cubans that will hurt them?" I ask.

Lukyan answers immediately. "The Plaza."

"Don't be an idiot," Evgeniy snaps. "It's basically impenetrable. An island surrounded by machine guns? You'd have to be suicidal to hit it."

"You'd have to be a coward not to."

"Shut up and let me think," Evgeniy says. He's quiet for a moment, then he says, "What about La Bamba?"

Lukyan rolls his eyes. "La Bamba is a down-and-out two-room 'casino' where all the washed-out Cubans end up so they can spend the last dregs of their pensions on cheap hookers and rigged slots. We might as well have a fruit fly massacre."

Evgeniy has taken to pacing around the circuit of the room, muttering quietly to himself. Halfway through, he stops and spins on his heel to face us again.

"El Palacio," he says triumphantly. His eyes dance with the fires of that deep-seated violence. He has Bratva blood in his veins—it just takes some stirring up, I think.

"El Palacio," Lukyan murmurs under his breath, like he's tasting the possibility. "Yeah, that could work. El Palacio. That's where they go after their late-night poker games, to blow off steam. High rollers, inner circle shit." He turns to look at me. "Does that meet your criteria, Bastien?"

I nod. "We'll hit it tonight and we'll hit it hard. Ready your men."

Evgeniy looks alarmed. "Hold on: you mean *tonight* tonight?"

I let my wordless look speak for itself.

Lukyan starts to cackle. "Shit yeah! Now, *this* is what I signed up for. This is what I signed up for! One of the legendary Nikolaev brothers himself, leading the charge. Hell fucking yes."

He pulls out his phone and gets texting.

"You," I say to Evgeniy, gesturing at the bodies strewn around us, "find out who these civilians were. Contact their families and make sure they're looked after. The Bratva leaves no man, woman, or child behind."

The odd hollow look in Evgeniy's eyes seems to lessen as he gets to his feet. Maneuvering in the shadows is what he does best. This job is right for him, and it takes something significant off my plate. That way, I can focus on what matters: hitting the Cubans where it hurts.

Amidst the strewn tables, smashed plates, and corpses in the restaurant below, the Bratva men we brought with us stand to attention. They're too far away to have heard much of what we said, but the vibe is unmistakable. The air is electric with motion, decision, action.

With danger.

With death.

Tonight will be a night to remember.

3

BASTIEN

I direct my attention out the window, watching as our SUV inches along the traffic-crammed highway. Cars pushed bumper to bumper, so close you could get out and walk along their roofs. That route would probably get us to El Palacio faster, actually.

Down the median, palm trees sway under the wind. Concrete slabs of buildings line the sidewalks as far as the eye can see. Up above, an invisible moon is out there somewhere.

The night is sweltering. Then again, every night in Miami is sweltering.

Evgeniy wrings his hands in his lap as he starts speaking. "About before... I shouldn't have—what I said back there, I didn't mean..." He splutters into silence uncomfortably.

"How old?" I ask quietly.

He turns to look at me, forehead wrinkled in confusion. "How old what?"

"How old were you when you first wanted out?"

He does a double-take at that. "I didn't. I don't..."

Then he sees in my eyes that he's already been exposed and he drops the lie. He's lucky Lukyan is in the other car right now.

"Twelve," he whispers, head hung low. "Papa said it was just a phase. I was such a good shot, he thought—actually, everyone thought... Fuck me, I don't know what I'm saying. It doesn't matter, anyway. I have to do what has to be done. Do honor by the Bratva. They're my family. My life."

"Might be time for a break," I suggest.

"What? No!" he balks immediately. His scowl almost turns into something different before he catches it. "My father was just killed. I can't quit now. The men, they need..." He shakes his head. "Papa would be so ashamed. And Lukyan would go ballistic."

I shrug and let the topic fade away. I'm not my cousin's therapist or his shoulder to cry on. I'm here for one reason and one reason only: to right the wrong. Slaughter the Cubans, get revenge, regain control.

Anything else is simply a distraction.

"Tell me about El Palacio," I say instead.

Evgeniy swallows, like he's glad we're putting the uncomfortable conversation behind us and focusing on nuts-and-bolts strategy.

"It's gonna be open season as soon as we kick the doors down. Every person in that shithole is a Cuban or owned by one." He pulls up a picture on his phone. "This is what it looks like."

I take it in with a grimace. The place is repulsive. Red-lit mirror walls, for fuck's sake. Leave it to the Cubans to make even a high-end strip club look like Tijuana trash.

But there's a tactical reason for my disgust, too. It means that aiming won't be easy. It's tough to have conviction pulling the trigger when the movement you're aiming at might just be your own damn reflection.

Everything else looks straightforward enough. For now. I wouldn't put it past José to have some more tricks up his sleeve, though.

Evgeniy lets out a nervous laugh. "This hit should be just the thing. Put an end to this."

He doesn't sound convinced.

Good. He shouldn't be.

We've been in the game long enough to know better. One good hit isn't going to finish off a strong power like the Cubans. They've been a fixture here for decades. It's going to take a lot more than that, no matter how many high-level Cuban *pridurki* we wipe out.

But it's a start. The first crippling of many to come.

I didn't choose an immediate attack on a Cuban-crammed spot to do anything less. This will be fast and merciless and effective.

That's how I like to work.

Over the past year, I've been working under my brothers, in New York and Boston. Skilled men whose skill transformed footholds into empires.

But men with their own methods. Methods I wouldn't necessarily have chosen.

Now, down here, I call the shots.

And tonight, the shots I'm calling are to gather as many dead Cubans as I can, as fast as I can get them.

Just then, my phone goes off. I answer without looking. Only a few people in the world have this number. And only one of them calls without warning.

"Bastien," Mother says, her tone scolding already.

I scowl. "This is not a good time."

"Perhaps if you'd answered my calls these past few days, then I wouldn't have had to call again," she asserts.

"Is there something that you want?"

"Is that how you speak to the woman who gave you life?"

I exhale. "I only have a few minutes. If you want something, get to it."

"That will do," she says tersely.

"Very well," I say. "What is it?"

"I heard there was some action. I wanted to ensure that you're okay."

"As you can no doubt hear, I'm fine," I say patiently.

Mother makes a dismissive noise. "Please, Bastien. Promise me you are unharmed."

"We arrived too late to help," I explain. "The only action my gun saw was being shoved in my back pocket, still fully loaded."

"You're sure?" she says suspiciously.

"Shouldn't you be checking up on Gavriil?" I ask coolly. "He's going crazy with baby planning and those prenatal courses Shannon has Hannah taking."

"Those prenatal courses were my idea," Mother says sharply. "And don't change the subject. You're stubbornly close-lipped. Do you remember when you were nineteen, you practically died of pneumonia right under my nose because you refused to take medicine and wrote it off as a bad cold?"

"Mother—"

"So it's perfectly reasonable for me to check in to make sure that you really are okay."

"And I'm telling you I'm fine."

"I may come for a visit, you know," she says in a friendly tone that we both know is more of a threat. "I do love Miami at this time of year."

"I wouldn't recommend it."

"And why not?"

"It's still volatile down here. You heard about that hit. It was at one of our restaurants. That, right after Uncle Maski... not many places are safe anymore."

"Hm. And the women in your life?"

"Are much the same as they were in Boston and New York," I finish in an even tone. "Irrelevant."

I can hear her snort in disbelief. I'm not lying, though. I haven't had much time to prowl Miami for an easy fuck. Bigger fish to fry.

"Of course, right now you're busy," she says, "but once things are settled..."

"Don't," I snap. My teeth grit. I know where this is leading. All too well.

"Is it too much for a mother to want all her sons to be nice and settled with good girls?" she demands. I can almost see her dark eyes flashing with self-righteousness.

"Right now, yes."

"Bastien Borya Nikolaev."

"Mother." All my patience was exhausted minutes ago. "Uncle Maksi called me here himself. He's dead. I have to help my cousins and the men we have here. That is my only priority. That's how this business works."

"Don't lecture me about how this business works, *moy syn*. I've been in it since you were just a twinkle in your father's eye." She pauses, then adds, "Once business is handled, then what? What comes after?"

I don't even bother coming up with an answer. There's too much riding on this hit for me to let anything else into my brain. Certainly not a fucking woman.

"'After' is still not assured," I growl. Then I hang up.

Beside me, Evgeniy's doing a poor job of pretending not to eye me thoughtfully.

"We all have family bullshit," I say shortly, to spare him the trouble.

"I get it," he says. "My mom's still trying to set me up the few times I see her. She's written Lukyan off as a lost cause, but since I'm 'such a nice boy'..."

I eye him. I don't say what I'm thinking. What I've heard. What I know he's done.

"It's true, you know," he says, somehow reading the silence. "What you heard."

"How do you know what I've heard?"

He chuckles darkly, although there's a sad note in it. "You had to have. Everyone knows and still brings it up time to time. It's like the setup to a bad joke."

"A Cuban girl," I say grimly. "What were you thinking?"

He nods. "You must think I'm an idiot," he sighs. "Even more than you do already."

I say nothing, just wait for him to explain.

"We didn't know at first," he says quietly, looking down at his shined shoes. "It was just some hookup in some dive bar. We didn't even exchange names, it all happened so fast." He laughs bitterly. "Goes without saying: I was an idiot. Wanted to keep her from the truth, so I could keep being the great, simple man she saw me as. Things grew from there, we got more serious, until the truth slapped us in the face so hard that my head is still ringing. I should've figured out myself that it was too good to be true."

He chuckles sadly again. "Lukyan was the one who found out what she was. A Cuban girl. Her daddy was a bigshot, high on the food chain. Not José himself, of course, just a cousin, but the difference didn't really matter. My brother claimed she was a spy; she swore it wasn't true. She'd never asked me about my business, never did anything suspicious, but I didn't know what to believe. By the time I got my head out of my ass, it was too late. She'd given up on me."

"A real Romeo and Juliet story," I say.

"I guess things could've ended up worse," Evgeniy says with a thoughtful shrug of his big shoulders. "I could be dead. But after that, I just didn't have the energy for that kind of stuff anymore. Relationships, going through the charade, pretending to be someone I'm not, until the inevitable disappointment. How could she not be, when I'm so fucking disappointed in myself already?"

He falls silent, patting at his pocket to check that his gun's still there.

"Sorry. I shouldn't have gone on like that. I don't know what got into me."

But I do: it's me.

Quiet people who listen are a rarity, Father once told me. Experience has proven it true. Just like now. Evgeniy talked and kept talking because, up until now, there hadn't been anyone who'd listen.

Not truly.

"What about you?" he asks. "Is that why you're holding out? Some big love story gone wrong?"

"Something like that," I say quietly.

He wants to say more, but leaves it. Good timing, too, because just then, we pull up a block from our destination.

Show time.

"You heard Lukyan," I tell our black-clothed men as they pile out of our SUVs, guns at the ready. "You stay in formation, shoot fast, and come on hard. We don't need survivors; we need to send a message. A very fucking bloody one."

Lukyan nods, eyes gleaming. The rest of the men follow suit.

Then we're off.

I stride up first. My men stay in the shadows a few paces behind, as instructed. The bouncer is a big, beefy guy. Looks like a professional wrestler. He slips to the ground like a wisp of feather when my bullet finds the center of his forehead.

I smile grimly as I step over his prone body and gesture to my men behind me to continue the advance. We push through the mirrored doors.

Further in, loud conversation and saucy music still reigns. They haven't realized who's here yet. Haven't realized what's about to happen.

In the entrance now, though, there's no one, except—

Movement. To the left. A hand, a gun, then *BAM,* I fire and my bullet turns that hand into a cloud of red mist.

The man attached to it howls in agony. My next bullet shuts him up forever.

Two Cubans down, a roomful more to go.

My men step up alongside me and filter throughout the room with tactical, practiced precision. All conversation has gone dead, but the music keeps booming as loud as ever.

Good. I like having a soundtrack to the bloodbath.

As for the Cubans themselves, some are scrambling, some are shooting, and some are still gaping at us, clueless. We start shooting them all.

Chaos erupts. Screams. Crashes. Shouts. But the place is rife with hiding spots, and after an initial onslaught, we find ourselves in a back-and-forth firefight.

Slowly, we chop through the defenses and advance into the main room. It's the one from the picture Evgeniy showed me: red-lit mirror walls, blue and black tiled floors.

I sense more motion and drop down, just as a bullet aimed for my head whistles over me. I shoot the shooter. The old man topples like a sack of potatoes.

I shoot wherever I see movement, wherever the darkness seems too broad or too dense. Beside me, my men have kept the line, as ordered.

Everywhere my bullets go, a body falls. They don't talk about this. The twisted bliss of this kind of work is like a drug to me. The clarity. The focus.

Ripping apart our enemy, bullet... by bullet... by bullet. Corpse by corpse by corpse.

Cleaning up the filth.

It's my Uncle Maksi I think about as I shoot them all: old and young, runners or shooters, the yellers and the quiet ones. Anything Cuban dies.

Maksi deserved better than what he got.

A young guy with a thin, sneering face points a gun into my chest. I laugh as mine goes off in his first.

Uncle Maksi, who cried when he spoke at Father's funeral. Who knew and loved the man who raised me like they were blood brothers.

Uncle Maksi, who was all we had left of Father.

This is for Uncle Maksi, you fucks.

This is for Father.

This is for anyone who ever dares to challenge the Bratva.

At some point, I stop seeing movement, stop hearing bullets. Lukyan and his men have advanced from the side door, and it looks like we've cleared out the room. The only remaining Cubans are the ones dying on the floor.

Lukyan storms over and nudges me with a scowl, eyeing one of the dead. "I know these men. All low-ranking. Fucking pond scum."

"You sure?"

He swings a look around, scowl deepening. "Yeah, I'm sure. Fuck."

I turn away, itching for something else to shoot. The whole fucking point of this was to hit the Cubans where it'd hurt them. Killing some low-ranking nobodies won't do shit.

Fuck is right.

"What do we do now?" Evgeniy wonders as he steps up to join us. He gestures to the club.

I pause, take it all in. The bodies. The saucy cumbia song still blaring overhead. The blood spatters that match the red of the mirror walls.

One big fucking waste.

If we leave now, this will all be for nothing. Within days, the Cubans, like industrious little ants, will return and rebuild. They'll have this place up and running in a month, tops.

Maybe this wasn't the big, crippling hit I'd intended, but I'll be damned if I leave this shithole for the Cubans to bring back to life.

"Burn it," I order.

Lukyan grins. Evgeniy pales.

"But one thing first," I say, heading for the back.

Maybe this trip was a waste, but perhaps if I can find something in an office, information of some kind...

In the back, I find two doors. One opens onto a bathroom where some Cuban went to die, slumped into the sink, like rinsing under the faucet could help fix the missing chunk of his face.

The other door leads to a kind of oversized closet. Cement walls and floors, two shitty plastic chairs. A scraped-top table, and...

I freeze.

So does the girl inside.

She looks early twenties, sandy blonde hair, green eyes, pouting lips... and the look she fixes on me glitters with defiance.

"Do your worst," she hisses in a throaty voice before I can even say anything. "I'm not going to beg."

I eye her. She's scared, of course. She'd have to be insane not to be. And yet, she's hiding it well.

It would be impressive, if I cared about such things. Staring death in the eye is not for the faint of heart.

And she would be attractive, if I cared about other such things. Tempting. Delicious.

But I don't care in either regard. I came here with a job to do. So this —however surprising—doesn't change that.

I pull out my gun and aim it at her face. "Unfortunately," I tell her, "I can't leave witnesses."

4

MELISSA

It's him.

Six foot five and towering. Black long-sleeved shirt on an insanely muscular torso. Dark, close-cut hair, pretty-boy brown eyes, and full lips wearing a brutal expression that seems far too cruel for a man so beautiful.

Bastien fucking Nikolaev.

Head enforcer of the Nikolaev Family.

None of those observations, however, change the fact that I'm about to die.

It's written in the hard lines on his sculpted face. A face that has seen and done much, much worse than kill some Cuban whore in the back of a club.

Despite how pointless it is, I open my mouth to make my pitch: *Take me with you; I'm a slave here; the Cubans killed my family when I was twelve and took me as a twisted prize.*

But then I see what his other hand is going for, and my lips fall shut as I practically keel over with relief.

Handcuffs.

Thank God.

"Turn around," he growls, catching my eye.

"Ask nicely first."

My shoulders jump at the sarcasm in my voice. Do I have a death wish? Guys like Bastien Nikolaev aren't exactly renowned for their sense of humor.

"Careful," he snarls. He advances toward me. His breath is hot against my neck as he closes the cuffs around my wrists.

"Or what?"

The unmistakable nozzle of a gun digs into my lower back. "Want me to spell it out for you?" he snaps.

"I've had a loaded gun pointed to my head, sorry," I blurt before I can stop myself. "You'll have to do better than that."

Bastien stalks in front of me, eyeing me. Maybe to confirm that, yes, I'm as psycho as I'm acting.

And yet, maybe it's wishful thinking, but is that a hint of a smile glimmering at the corner of his mouth?

"Go on," he goads. "Continue. See how you like a gag between those pretty lips."

A weird shiver that can't decide whether it's terrified or inappropriately turned on rips through me. *At least Murder Boy thinks I have pretty lips?*

I drop my chin to my chest and start to hum to myself. The same song I was singing just before this angel of death burst in here for God-knows-what kind of reason.

Te regalo mi cintura... Y mis labios para cuando quieras besar...

Why am I singing? Why am I sassing? Excellent questions. The only answer I can think of is that maybe the terror has finally cracked me. Maybe a lifetime of evil men doing evil things to my body has finally caught up.

"Your voice is beautiful," Bastien mutters in surprise. His scowl deepens when he realizes he's spoken aloud. "But shut up. Final warning."

I raise my eyes to him. "What difference does it make?"

"I need to concentrate."

"On?" I use my shoulder to gesture around at our empty surroundings. "I'm the one in handcuffs, not you."

His gaze slants my way, and, though I recognize what's burning in it, I don't recognize what's happening inside me.

When he doesn't respond, I continue, "Really, I'm not strong. Or fast. More like the definition of a non-threat. If anyone should be concentrating, it's me, since I don't know what you're going to do with me. Or what you did here."

I pause and notice how eerily silent the club is. "Did you kill everyone?"

Bastien quirks a brow. He's still wearing that expression that's halfway between an amused smirk and a damning scowl.

"I don't care, really," I say. "I mean, I do, but not in the way you think. Anyway, if you're going to kill me, won't you just tell me? You owe me that, at least."

Another brow quirk. Yeah, let's get real here: Mr. Brooding Russian doesn't owe me jack-shit.

But I can't shut up. Out of fear or attraction or stupidity—who the hell knows at this point—I keep blabbering like a moron who wants to swallow a bullet.

"Suit yourself," I say. "We can stand here talking all day until the police show up. That suits me just fine."

Bastien's gaze is flat, revealing nothing.

"What?" I say. "For fuck's sake, say something!"

"Do you always tempt fate like this?" he murmurs.

"No," I admit. "You must have caught me on a good day. Lucky you."

A smirk lifts the right side of his mouth. "We'll see who's the lucky one soon enough."

Gripping me by the handcuffs, he yanks me along after him. As if I needed any more reminding that I'm the prisoner here.

He drags me back down the hallway. The one light bulb has gone out, so we're mired in gloom.

"What are you doing here?" I ask. I'm avoiding looking out there, into the heart of El Palacio. I'll say, do, or obey anything if it means I don't have to witness that bloodbath.

Part of me always imagined something like this happening. A white knight swooping in, slaying all my enemies, and freeing me, the princess in the castle.

But I'm no princess, and Bastien is sure as hell no white knight. The only thing my fantasy has in common with this grim reality is that everyone who's ever hurt me is dead.

Everyone who's ever hurt me *so far,* that is. It remains to be seen whether Bastien will join that list.

He still hasn't responded to my question. "Can I get something other than the silent treatment, please?"

"You should be glad that's all you get," he growls with a tug on my handcuffs.

I can hear others out there. His men, no doubt. His fellow slaughterers. Joking, stalking about, out there in the club amidst the carnage.

"You have a really inclusive definition of lucky," I say drily.

"And you seem not to value your life very much."

Is it insane that part of me is actually finding this fun? In a twisted, sad, I'm-maybe-about-to-die-and-my-life-was-dead-monotonous-before way. I guess this is why they call it gallows humor. Everyone gets funnier when there's nothing left to lose.

"What's your name?" he says, almost as an afterthought.

He stands beside me, not looking at me. Does that make this easier for him, too?

"I know yours," I blurt out. "Bastien Nikolaev."

He swings to look at me, tilting up my chin so I'm looking him right in his glaring eyes. "Then you know I'm an impatient kind of man."

"Try 'vicious murderer' and you'll be closer to the truth," I sneer. I try to jerk my chin away from his heated touch, but he holds me there for a few seconds as if to remind me who's in charge.

When I finally stop struggling, he lets his hand drop. "And you're some sort of angel? Working here, doing what you do?"

"Being a dancer is a far cry from being a killer."

He shrugs. "We all do what needs to be done."

"You can't be serious."

"Haven't you sinned, little one?" he whispers.

"I haven't committed murder, that's for damn sure."

A shudder goes through me. *Liar*, a quiet vicious voice hisses in my head. *Filthy fucking liar.*

He scowls, still waiting. I shudder and repress the nightmarish memory threatening to boil up inside of me.

"Anyway," I continue, "that's assuming that I'm a dancer by choice. Which is not the case."

At that, he swings a curious look my way. I stare back at him. I don't need his pity.

Not that I'm seeing anything remotely like sympathy in his eyes. They have a studied flatness to them that I'm sure girls more sympathetic than me haven't been able to penetrate. A kind of dark sheen that says quite clearly, *Fuck off.*

"You should be happy then," he says, nodding to the out-there I still haven't dared glance at. "You're free of them."

"Happy isn't the word I'd use," I whisper.

He doesn't say anything, and I don't try to explain. How can I? Only if he were trapped here would he have understood, and even then he might not.

Maybe the Cubans wouldn't have broken him if he were in my shoes. Maybe he would've died, proud and free and hating every last one of them.

How can I explain that, come what may, after all the Cubans did to me, the one thing I've been good at holding to is the will to live?

And in order to do that, I couldn't hate all the Cubans, even though they were all in on all of it—my enslavement, what happened to my parents, what they did to me.

I hated Raul and José and the men who pawed at me and acted like I was some animal who had to take it, sure.

But some of the others had kindness in them.

And now, it's spilling out of them, one thick red drop at a time.

Bastien's low voice breaks me out of my reverie. "What then?"

"Huh?"

"What word would you use?"

I try to cross my arms across my chest, forgetting the handcuffs. They cut into my skin and jangle. "I don't know. It doesn't matter."

It suddenly annoys me how I've been a complete open book to this killer I met minutes ago. I stand there, glaring down at my feet, alternating between angry and afraid, hot and cold, feeling safer than I've ever felt at the same time that I wonder if the man at my side is the most violent danger yet.

My nails are the same purple glitter polish that Kayla and I did the other week. Seems like a lifetime ago already.

I stand there, waiting for him to say something, do something. Out in the club, there's the sounds of low conversation, the odd chuckle, objects shifting.

In this dark, dank hallway, it's just broody silence.

"What are we waiting for?" I finally ask.

"For things to calm down."

He doesn't answer. Anyone with ears can hear that the only sounds now are random grunts and unworried chitchat. And anyone with eyes can probably see that nobody is left to…

No. I won't look.

My gaze falls back to my stilettos and toes. Kayla wasn't here tonight. Thank God for that. She, at least, was spared.

For whatever it's worth. Who knows if I'll even ever get to see her again?

Just then, we hear footsteps. I look up to see a short, stout man with a scowling face approach.

Seeing us at the last second, he does a double take. "Bastien?"

"I found this one," Bastien says simply, indicating me.

"Okay…" the man says. He's clearly waiting for more explanation.

Bastien offers none. "Any others?" he says instead, taking a step forward to crane his neck around the club.

"Nope," the man says grimly. "They might've been nobodies, but we at least finished them off good. It was a good hit."

His words—*finished them off good*—pierce through me like a bullet.

Tío Pedro, who for my birthday brought me my favorite vanilla cookies—finished off.

Tía Rodriga, who stopped José from sending me to work a street corner—finished off.

Antonia, who tried warning me earlier today to stay in line—finished off.

God, all the carefulness didn't help you in this, poor girl...

"A good hit in a bad place," Bastien mutters.

The man is eyeing me like I'm a puzzle piece that doesn't fit anywhere. Finally, he looks to Bastien. "So what now?"

Bastien starts moving, unhurried yet swift, tugging me along.

I can feel his soldiers' eyes snaking to me. Twin pinpricks in the darkness, like nighttime hunters. The eyes of dangerous men.

Just look at your feet, don't look up, just look at your stupid, sparkly, purple feet with the pretty silver rhinestone stilettos...

A shudder goes through me.

You can do this, you have to do this, just don't look, don't you dare look, and everything will be fine, and—oh God, I'm stepping over something; that's a body with a bullet in the center of his balding forehead; those are dead, unseeing pea-green eyes. He smells like the fruity drink splashed all over him and beneath that, a graveyard mold, a sickly-sweet scent that punches itself up my nostrils...

A low moan rolls out of me as my knees weaken.

"Now, we leave," Bastien says over his shoulder to the man without ever relinquishing his grip on my upper arm. "Our work here is done."

"Bastien..." the man says, with a tone that sounds like a warning.

Bastien ignores him. He keeps on walking as if he hadn't heard. I stagger alongside, feeling like I might vomit.

"Bastien," the man says again, and finally, the Nikolaev avenger comes to a stop.

Another man is blocking our path, a bigger, wider one ridged with muscles. His dark eyes have a watery sheen to them, almost as if...

Wait, no way. No way, right?

Trained killers wouldn't tear up at doing what they're trained to. These Bratva guys, from what I hear, live, sleep, and eat this life. They wake up craving death. They go to sleep sated with the death they've consumed.

But *feeling* anything for the destruction they've caused? Feeling pity, sorrow, emotion of any kind?

Not a fucking chance.

This man, though... There's no mistaking his tears.

"Evgeniy," Bastien sighs.

"Who is that?" Evgeniy asks, eyeing me. A bead of sweat trickles down his sad face.

"A nobody," Bastien says. "Just a dancer."

"A witness," the other man from before corrects, having caught up to us. There's no doubt about the tone in his voice. It's damning. A death sentence. *Finish her off like the rest,* he's saying.

"She was in the back," Bastien retorts. "Didn't see anything."

"He's right," I blurt. "Under a table. I didn't see a damn—"

"Shut up," Bastien growls, giving me a shake via the handcuffs. "I didn't tell you to speak."

I can see why: the one man's eyes are narrowed, while the other, Evgeniy, is already looking away.

"Bastien," the first man says, "think this through. She heard everything. She just walked through what we did here. She's a witness. We can't have a witness going to the police and blabbing what happened here."

My heart is beating so fast and hard it feels like it might just tumble out of my chest and make a run for the door all by itself.

"She's not going anywhere, Lukyan," Bastien snaps back.

"She needs to be put down."

Bastien doesn't say anything. Is that because his mind is made up or because he's actually mulling it over?

Oh God, no...

"Listen to me, cousin," Lukyan continues. "She's clearly—"

"Not one of them," Bastien interrupts. "No need for her to share their fate."

Lukyan's face is tight, impassive, and cruel. "First chance she gets, she'll be running to the police."

"I've been held here for ten years and I've never tried escaping, not once," I cut in, my words falling over each other because I'm trying to get them out so fast. "I've never blabbed. I've never talked to a cop. Let me go and I'll just disappear."

Bastien, Lukyan, Evgeniy—they have to listen. They have to see.

I can't die. Not now, not like this. Not after all I've been through.

Evgeniy can't seem to look anywhere, while Lukyan is already shaking his head. "She could be lying."

"If I have prisoners, they stay prisoners," is all Bastien says.

"So that's it?" Lukyan demands. "You're committing to keeping her locked up for the rest of her life? That's your decision?"

"Until we find a solution, yes."

"No." Lukyan shakes his head. "You know how this works. We can't endanger the Bratva like that."

"We don't kill women," Bastien says, mouth curved into a feral snarl. "Ever."

Now, Evgeniy is the one to speak bitterly. "The dead girl in the corner would suggest otherwise."

"I can't control stray bullets," Bastien says. "Or what my men do in a fury. But I will not shoot a woman point-blank in cold blood."

Lukyan lifts his gun, points it at me, and clicks off the safety. "No one said *you* had to pull the trigger."

Oh shit, I'm going to die. That's it. I'm going to, going to, going to—

Viper-fast, Bastien's hand shoots out, grabs the muzzle, and points it away. "Don't you ever aim your gun in my direction, *tupitsa*."

"I thought you were tougher than this," Lukyan sighs. He's still clinging stubbornly to the gun.

"My family has rules," Bastien rumbles. "Ethics. A code."

"We aren't in New York," Lukyan says quietly. "Or Boston."

I'm not safe yet. *Mama, if you're listening, I just want you to know that I love you, and that I'm sorry, I'm so, so sorry—*

"Cousin. Brother," Evgeniy says to each of them, looking about as sick as I'm feeling. "Maybe we can come up with some sort of compromise?"

"Like what?" Lukyan barks out a derisive laugh, throwing his head back before fixing a deadly, blue-eyed gaze on me. "Only half-kill her? Cut out her tongue?"

I'm shaking and I can't stop.

"Don't be a fool," Bastien hisses.

"I could say the same to you," Lukyan bites back.

Evgeniy sighs. "Maybe we could decide later?"

"Shut up, Evgeniy," they chorus simultaneously. It's clearly an accident, but I can't help laughing at the absurdity of it. Like this is all scripted. Pre-planned. Like my fate has already been decided and we're just bantering until the audience is ready to see more blood.

"Enough of this," Lukyan snarls. "I'm making the call myself."

It happens so fast.

It's one smooth motion, really, so fast and seamless that I only realize what's happened after I hear the shot.

With his other delicate hand, Lukyan takes out another gun.

Aims it at me.

And fires.

5

BASTIEN

The shot slices the air.

It misses—barely. Mere inches from the girl's head.

Then it's my turn. And I never miss.

I barrel into Lukyan, taking him down in a savage tackle. We hit the ground hard. As he bucks against me, I rip his arms back and press the flat of my palm into his throat.

Right into his face, I growl, "The girl lives. That's final."

Two more bucks follow, him wheezing furiously, before he realizes he doesn't stand a chance. He sinks to the ground, gaping up at me.

I relinquish my hold on his windpipe. "Do you understand, Lukyan?"

He breathes hard, saying nothing.

"Do. You. Understand?" I enunciate.

His blue eyes are veiny with angry red. He clearly didn't expect this—my strength. My speed. My ferocity. He thought those were just embellished stories people told about me.

I bare my teeth at him in a wolfish snarl. *Should've known better, cousin.*

I didn't inherit my reputation like some old family trinket. I earned every fucking bit of it myself. Through study, through training, through time in the heat of battle.

I've been tested and passed. Him? He just thinks he knows what tough is.

I've lived it. I *am* it.

He won't make that mistake again.

"Cousin," Lukyan manages to breathe, repentance obvious in the gaping slackness of his mouth.

He still wonders: *Will I kill him?*

I'm not quite sure, myself.

"If you slaughter an innocent girl, what makes us any better than the Cubans?" I hiss.

Around us, the men have quieted, are watching. It makes no difference to me. This is between Lukyan and myself. Everyone else is merely a witness to what it means to truly be Bratva.

My cousin's forehead crinkles. "Bastien, you can't be saying that—"

I remove my hand from his sweaty neck and climb off. But I'm not done with him just yet.

I tower over him, casually passing my gun from one hand to the other. It's implicit: one more act of disobedience will cost him his life. I didn't come down this this alligator-infested swamp to sit back and watch others screw things up.

I came to take fucking charge.

"We were here first," Lukyan stutters out. "They killed our father; they have no honor—"

"There, that's it." I look at him hard. "The Cubans have no honor. So therefore, it makes no fucking difference who was here first, or even that they are Cubans and we are Russian. The only law of power is that the strongest wins. But as for why we should, why we deserve to make Miami ours... why bother if the result is the same either way?"

Lukyan blinks at me, stumped. He was born and bred on the idea that every city we wanted was ours by mere birthright. That there need be no better reason for our control.

I came to a different conclusion.

Evgeniy chimes in like he thinks I'm on his side. "Bastien is right. All this murder and destruction... for what purpose?"

He's wrong, though—I'm not on his side. I'm on no one's side but my own.

"The purpose is to put the city in the right hands," I say. I put away my gun. I can see I won't be needing it now. "We are the right hands—as long as we stick to certain principles. I don't know what keeps you fighting, cousins, and I don't care. But I know for me, it's this recognition of our superiority that makes it worth it. We have honor and the Cubans do not. Our honor may be inconvenient at times, even a weakness that our enemies can and have exploited. But it is what makes all this worthwhile. Makes the promise of a better future under us a real one. We will not kill or harm the innocent. We will take care of those who put their trust in us. *And we do not kill innocent women.*"

It's quiet in here. The quiet of listening, not necessarily understanding.

I eye my cousin, still slopped on the floor, all sweaty-faced and slack-jawed. He's unsure whether to be scared or confused or just tired.

But I'm done explaining myself. If he doesn't get it, that's on him.

If you're in charge, there should be a damn good reason why: because you place honor above everything. Principles above everything. Duty and loyalty above everything.

No hesitation. No weakness. Nothing but necessity.

Lukyan sees all this in my eyes and exhales. I'm still so close to him I can smell his sweat, fresh and strong. "Shit, cousin, I—"

"Fucked up," I finish for him.

He nods, admitting his error. "But what will we do with her if we're not killing her?"

I don't look at the girl, who hasn't said a word since Lukyan pulled the trigger. It'll just be an unnecessary distraction.

A plan is already forming in my head already as I open my mouth. There's only one thing to do.

"I'll keep her prisoner myself until I can figure out something better," I say quietly.

Lukyan is silent. He doesn't need to state the obvious: that this is a fucking liability. An ongoing problem without an obvious solution.

He's still struggling with the desire to say something. He's questioning whether to take my word as law or to keep pushing back.

He'd better choose very goddamn carefully.

"Is that okay with you?" I drawl, laced with sarcasm. "Or would you prefer to settle this a different way?"

"I wasn't—I would never—" Lukyan protests, red face going white.

"You defied a direct order," I remind him. "I told you no. You fired anyway. I don't think I need to tell you how lucky you are that your aim is shit."

He swallows. His Adam's apple rides up and down. "I apologize, cousin," he says finally. "I just... tonight's got me pissed off. I was going in with high hopes that we'd get some big players and now..."

"Now, this," Evgeniy says quietly.

Throughout the club, the tension has eased. Our men have lost interest, started wandering, looting some more. Most are keeping a keen ear open for when I'll give the order to leave.

"I'm pissed off, too," I say. "But what's done is done. This won't be our last hit. And it certainly won't be our worst. Not if I get the intel I need and I end this war the way I intend to do."

For the first time since we came in here, Lukyan looks excited again.

"But," I say, "I can't do that without your full cooperation, cousin." I eye him like I'm still not sure what to do with him. Not sure I can trust him. Because I'm not, and because I don't think I can. "Do I have it?"

Lukyan exhales and, at long last, nods. "You have my full apology, Bastien. Papa would've been disgusted to see me fighting with a Nikolaev. He always spoke so highly of your father and you all."

I crouch to offer him a hand. "Then we're settled. Now, are you ready to go?"

Lukyan nods, taking my help a bit warily as he clambers back to his feet.

Behind me, the girl hasn't moved an inch. She's leaning against a pole like it's the only thing keeping her standing. Maybe it is. Can't be every day you see your workplace turned into rubble.

I eye the clear path to the door. Could she have tried escaping? Unlikely that Evgeniy was watching her. No one else knew who the hell she was until Lukyan made a fuss. Amidst all the chaos, how hard would it have been to slip out the side...?

But she's here. She stayed.

I smirk. It means she's not a complete idiot, even if she does babble. We're about to find out what else she might be.

For now, though, it's time to go.

Our work here is finished.

6

BASTIEN

The night outside the car windows is moonless and dark. The streets are empty. Lukyan and Evgeniy made the turn to the headquarters a few minutes ago. I kept on going.

"Thank you for not killing me," she murmurs from the passenger seat.

I let her words sit. An outstretched hand I won't take. Right now, there's no need to talk. Just to get her to my place.

Concentrate.

"And for not letting him kill me, either. You saved my life."

No shit. Still, no need to respond. That way lies danger.

Just concentrate.

"Do you hear—" she starts.

Fucking hell. Might as well get this fucking over with.

"It had nothing to do with you," I snarl. "You heard me. My brothers and I, my men, we live by a code. Whether the Limonovs do or not is not my fucking concern. Now that I'm here, my code takes precedence. My word takes precedence. My orders take precedence."

I curse as soon as I'm finished with the mini-tirade. What is it about this girl that keeps making me say more than I intended?

"Now, be quiet," I add.

Another silence follows, almost as if she's testing something. Or maybe she's finally got the goddamn hint.

"I'm Melissa, by the way," she says. "You asked me my name earlier, but I didn't get the chance to tell you."

I don't respond. Knowing anything about her will only complicate matters. I intend to rid myself of this problem sooner, not later. No point in making it thornier in the meantime.

I crank the air-conditioning to the highest setting. It emits a low drone. The blasts of cool air on my face are almost calming.

I can see Melissa's eyes straying to the radio. I heard her sing to herself when I barged into the back. She must be one of those people who uses music like a security blanket.

I prefer silence.

Driving quietly helps me focus. Helps me think. It's why I dispensed with a chauffeur, why I insisted on driving the two of us back to my house myself.

Besides, a Bratva driver would just be another distraction, another potential liability. The fewer people who know where I live, the better.

"Bastien…" she begins.

Ah, for fuck's sake. There she goes ruining the moment.

I wheel the car off to the shoulder, cut the engine, and round on her. "Listen to me and listen very fucking closely, little one. Just because

I'm not killing you doesn't mean that things are going to be easy for you." I lean in closer so she can see just how much I mean every word I'm saying, getting an inhale of her scent in the process. *Is that guava?* I think idly. "You need to keep your mouth shut and obey every goddamn word I say until I decide what I'm going to do."

She stares at me, her eyes two green slits of defiance.

This little fucking minx.

She needs a lesson in manners. One I'm just dying to give her. I want to grab her and show her, show her how much I mean every word, show her what's required of her: absolute submission.

But I can see that it will take time.

Because when she speaks, her voice is laced with derision. "Things aren't going to be easy for me? Please. They can't be worse than when I was with the Cubans, *Bastien.*"

I flinch. I'm already despising when she uses my name like we're on a first-name basis. Like we're anything more than captor and captured.

Like she has any sort of say in her fate.

I smile. It isn't a nice one. "Can't be worse?" It's a test, a dare, a threat —and she knows it.

She sticks out her chin anyway, eyes flashing. "Not a chance."

I just shake my head slowly. "If there's one thing I can promise you, *kotyonok,* it's this: I'm the only man alive who can always, always make things worse. So, if you think you're safer with me than with the Cubans, then you're wrong. Dead wrong. I've spared you thus far. As for what happens next? That is up to you."

Her lips fell open, slackened. I just tore away the last lifeline she had.

Good. It's about time she finally grasped the reality of all this.

"What you need to do right now is shut your mouth and do what you're told," I say finally, starting up the car again.

I've made my point. Whether it was out of necessity or desire is another matter entirely.

I can't say I feel nothing when I look at Melissa, that there isn't some sort of chemistry. *That golden hair, those pert tits and teasing lips, the insolent flash in those evergreen eyes...*

It has an effect I won't deny. Crackles all the way to my hardened cock.

But I know where it would lead: absolutely fucking nowhere. I can't let things between us get out of control. I can't let what happened to Nina happen to her.

I'll do whatever it takes—even worse than what I did to Nina.

If you're in charge, there better be a damn good reason why.

And my reason is this: I don't make the same mistake twice.

I aim my eyes on the road, grab the steering wheel, turn back onto the highway and get driving. It takes a few silent minutes for me to notice the reason for the bolts of feeling running down my thumbs and fingers—I'm gripping the steering wheel so hard my knuckles are white.

The whole fucking car smells like guava, like her. I open a window to smell literally anything else.

Maybe I should take Lukyan up on his constant offers and get a Bratva woman to take the edge off. Or just go to a nightclub and find someone to fulfill the purpose. God knows Miami is full of willing women who part their legs readily for men like me.

But for now, right now, I just need to not think about it. About any of it.

Like how my cock could teach her the best manners of all: shut up and listen.

Like whether her eyes would keep that insolent gleam right up to the moment she shattered on my dick.

Like how she'd sound when that happened. A whimpering little moan, a full-throated cry—what would it be?

Fuck's sake, Bastien, focus on the fucking road.

At some point, she starts singing. It's another Spanish song I don't know the words to.

Not that I need to. With that low, throaty voice, her singing out her grocery list would be beautiful. It's got a unique rasp that grips you. A sort of captivating sadness to it. Melancholy, amber-tinged.

Where did you learn to sing like that? is on the tip of my tongue before I shove it back down again.

I scowl, wrenching my eyes back on the road. We're almost there anyway. I don't need her life story. All I need is for her to understand who's in charge here.

A few minutes away from my place, I give my clothes—black t-shirt and dark gray jeans—a quick once-over for any telltale bloodstains. Not that I'm likely to see anyone, but it always pays to be ready for the unexpected.

I chose this house in the suburbs because it was innocuous, unexpected. The last place anyone would think to look for Bastien Nikolaev. The fact that it's affluent helps. Any idiot knows that if you hit a rich neighborhood, the police will be there faster than you can say, "Whoops." They know who pays their bills and votes in their elections.

Thankfully, there are no stains to be seen. Guess I still do neat work.

As we pull into my driveway, though, I pause, realizing we have a problem.

Melissa is still dressed like a stripper: a siren-red sequined bra and skirt that barely skims the top of her ass. It doesn't really matter, since we'll only be outside for as long as it takes to cross from the driveway to the front door.

But I don't want to risk blowing my cover so cheaply. There are eyes everywhere, always. It's best to act like your enemies are right on your ass. They may not look like enemies, they may not sound like enemies, but the only truth I care about is this: anyone who is not sworn Bratva is an enemy by definition.

So when I see a shape on the sidewalk, my nose wrinkles in irritation.

Of fucking course.

It's after midnight, when all the nice, wholesome residents in this nice, wholesome neighborhood should be asleep. And yet there he is— Randy Finch, the most wholesome family man of them all. He's walking his fat white sheepdog down the sidewalk. Already, he's stopping to wave as we approach.

Thank fuck the Range Rover has tinted windows and it's nighttime.

I rip open the glove compartment, grab a plaid blanket we keep in there for emergencies and toss it at Melissa. "Wrap this around yourself."

She blinks at me, almost smirking, then waggles her handcuffs like I'm slow in the head.

I growl, annoyed. It's not like me to forget something like that. Matter of fact, this whole damn night is not like me.

I hurriedly wrap her in the blanket, then get out and walk around to her side of the car to let her out.

When I glance up, Randy's halfway across the street, ambling in our direction. His belly strains against his baby blue Ralph Lauren polo shirt.

I'll say this for the motherfucker: he's determined. Determined to forge a neighborly bond with me despite my never giving him a single inclination that I'm interested in anything of the sort. The man brought me a plate of brownies the day I moved in here, for fuck's sake.

"Evening, Bastien!" he crows. Volume moderation is not his forte. Half the neighborhood can hear him.

I wince. "Randy," I greet coolly.

"What a night, eh?" The streetlights shine off the bald spot on his pasty head. "Molly's just loving it."

Molly—the furry sheepdog currently licking at my shoes—gives a delighted little tap-dance. Melissa giggles.

After hits like what we just did at El Palacio, it isn't the immediate aftermath that's the shock. It's trying to go out into the real world and act normal that jars the most. To buy a coffee, drive a car, unlock your front door.

Or, for instance, to talk to your intrusive neighbor.

"And who is this, might I ask?" Randy says, glancing over at Melissa.

My hands fist.

Here we go. Game time.

The question is…

How will Melissa behave?

7

MELISSA

"And who is this, might I ask?" says the chubby man in the polo.

"A friend," Bastien cuts in before I can think of how to describe myself. He jerks his head towards the dog. "How's the pup?"

Randy doesn't seem to realize that Bastien is obviously changing the subject. "Oh, you know, she's been better," he says with a rueful shake of his head. "Misses our Helen. They used to spend all their time together, but she's all set for a visit next month so it's not so bad!"

Bastien's jaw thrums with tension. "And Helen is…"

"Going to Penn State, yep," Randy confirms. He also doesn't seem to realize that Bastien doesn't have the faintest fucking idea who Helen is.

Seeing Bastien even tolerate this conversation is pretty funny, if I'm being honest. Like seeing a dog walk on its hind legs.

Bastien Nikolaev, infamous Bratva killer…

And also, a chit-chatty neighbor?

Strange role for him to play. But I have to remind myself that it's just that: a role. The real Bastien Nikolaev… is different, to say the least.

"Top of her class," Randy says with a proud nod of his flabby chin. "My baby's going to be a doctor."

"Good for her," Bastien says. Casually, he wraps a muscular arm around my shoulder.

It's not a kind or tender gesture. He's only doing it to stop me from turning around and making it obvious, blanket or no blanket, that my hands are cuffed behind my back. It's all just part of the role.

… Right?

I eye Randy. He is a suburbanite straight out of Central Casting. Bald, plump, innocuous. Could he really be exactly how he seems: a regular old, busybody neighbor out for a night walk with the pooch?

I think so. Then again, you probably wouldn't peg Bastien for a coldblooded killer if you just glimpsed him strolling into his house in the neighborhood here.

I turn my attention to the three- and four-story mansions lining the street around us. Every single one seems to come from a different period and school of architecture. There's an English Tudor across the street, a Spanish villa further on. Bastien's is more modern, while Randy's has a beachy sophistication to it.

The money here is obvious. But looking at all of these beautiful houses, all I can think about is the people they hold—and their secrets.

Pretty faces always hide the nastiest rot beneath.

Bastien's grip on my shoulder grows firmer. "You must be proud," he says to Randy, voice clipped.

"You, too, buster," Randy teases with the most dad-like *nudge-nudge* of the elbow I've ever seen. Just to make sure we all get what he's talking about, he looks at me and winks. "What did you say your name was, sweetheart?'

"I'm Melissa," I say with a grin. "Bastien's girlfriend. It's a pleasure to meet you."

The conversation drops dead. Bastien's smile grows brittle; Randy's just about covers his whole face. Mine is somewhere in between—I'm halfway to guffawing at how uncomfortable Bastien is, and halfway to wondering if I just made a terrible, terrible mistake.

"Pleasure is all mine!" he says, sticking out a hand.

I eye it warily. The handcuffs might be a problem after all.

Exchanging a look with Bastien, whose glare could slice cement, I force a laugh. "I'm not a big handshaker. Too much of a germaphobe, I'm afraid."

Randy chuckles and tucks his hand back in his pocket. "Ah well, my daughter would probably tell you that's good for your health," he says with a good-humored laugh. "Pre-med, don't ya know. Are you a picky eater, too? Amy's been hankering for me to have you over, Bastien, and I'm sure she'd love it if you came as well, Melissa. I feel like you two would get along famously with the ol' ball and chain."

"No," Bastien says—just as I say, "We'd love to!"

His grip gets so tense it's painful. I swallow back a whimper. And—far too little, far too late—a sudden gut-punch of dread. Because I've realized something: if Randy caught on to what was going on, would Bastien kill him?

You've got to be joking, Mel, drawls my inner cynic.

It should've been obvious: he wouldn't hesitate to put this fat bozo in the dirt.

Back in El Palacio, Bastien spoke eloquently enough about honor and a code, about not killing innocents. But at the end of the day, he'll do what needs to be done. Whatever that entails.

"My wife makes a mean lasagna. It's what made me fall in love with her in the first place, actually. When you try it, you'll understand. Although you better keep your hands to yourself!"

Another laugh, another nudge with the elbow. Bastien looks ready to implode. "Looking forward to it," he says tightly.

"Anyway," Randy says, as his dog yearns for a nearby grassy shoulder, "Molly'll be pulling my arm off if I make her wait any longer for this walk of hers. It was great talking with you both."

"You as well," Bastien says.

Finally, his grip on my shoulder starts to lessen. Until—

"Oh, almost forgot," Randy says, pausing a few steps away. "A date and time—how about this Friday?"

"Wonderful," Bastien grits.

"Great," Randy beams, bustling away with a wave. "Have a good night!"

Bastien keeps a claw on me until Randy rounds the corner, whistling. As soon as the man is out of sight, he's yanking me viciously to the stairs leading up to his black, windowless door.

He shoves me inside and slams the door behind me. Towering tall, eyes flashing, he growls, "What the hell was that?"

"It's called being a decent human being," I snap. I make to move past him. I'm not going to let him intimidate me, even if we are alone right now and I'm in handcuffs.

But he's having none of that.

With the flat of his palm, mouth twisted into a dangerous scowl, he shoves me right back into the door. The knob digs painfully into my back. "Try again."

"I would say I went with everything pretty well," I say, glaring right back up at him.

Struggling is useless, but I still try. Jesus, he is *strong*.

"Wrong again," he hisses. "You have no idea what you've just done."

I roll my eyes. "Forgive me, I should've known: with you Bratva boys, any simple conversation is loaded with consequences."

"You just put the entire street in danger. Yourself included. Nice old Randy Finch? He might just wake up with a bullet in his brain that his nice doctor daughter can't fix, thanks to you. Or he could even be a Cuban informant, and it's our heads that'll take the bullets. You stupid, stupid little girl."

I swallow and exhale. I'm trying to keep a brave face, even though there's some very real merit to what he's saying. "You're overreacting."

"I'm stating the facts," he retorts, emotionless. "If anybody learns you're here, and if the Cubans find out, you're going to be in for a world of pain. You and anyone else involved."

"Is that a threat?"

"Yes. But not from me."

Bastien takes a step back, looking at me with angry eyes. He almost convinces me, with this whole subdued-anger-slash-frustration thing.

Too bad I know more about the mob life and how men like him work than he thinks I do. Way more.

"Want to know what I think?" I say. "One: I think it just got a whole lot harder for you to kill me, even if you claim you were never going to, since we've been seen together now." I pause. "Come to think of it, that was the only point I had. Oh, wait, except for… it's worth it just to see you squirm."

His mouth twists into one of those dangerous scowls as he presses each hand against the wall on either side of me. "I wouldn't be so sure, *kotyonok*. Accidents happen. People get killed."

I shiver. How can you be scared of someone and awed by them at the same time?

"I'm a professional," he continues, arms hemming me in place. "It wouldn't be hard at all. Quite easy, really."

What would be easy would be giving into the look in those dark eyes. The problem is, once I do that, there's no coming back.

"As long as we play our roles," I say in a voice that is much, much less shaken than I actually feel, "then no one has to know who I really am."

Bastien's glare cuts into me so deep I'm almost surprised that I'm still standing here. He turns away before his scowl takes over his entire face, hands fisted. "You've got all the answers, don't you?"

I open my mouth to give yet another snappy comeback, but the words don't come. It's only then that I realize how tired I am.

I'm so tired. Bone-deep tired, soul-deep tired. Tired of being on my guard 24/7. Tired of trusting no one but Kayla. Tired of always searching, always waiting for that way out, that chance that had to come eventually. The chance that never has.

"No, I don't," I mumble. "I don't even know why you let me live."

"I told you—"

"I know, I know, the code. Fabulous. But why not saddle one of your men with the job of having me imprisoned and watched? Hell, I bet you have friends in the police. You could get me thrown into jail on trumped-up charges, no problem. You wouldn't have to kill me then. All you'd have to do is turn your back."

Bastien studies me carefully for a long time. "This way was easiest," he finally says. "The men here, I trust them, but… they still aren't my men, most of them. I brought a few from Boston, but the majority are Limonov boys. Mistakes can be made."

"So?" I say, a little baffled by his transparency. "I'm just another innocent bystander who got the shit end of the stick. Another unintended victim. What's it to you?"

"Not a damn thing," he says tersely. He lets his hands fall to his sides. "You're just a prisoner of war. Nothing more. Nothing less."

"If I'm a prisoner, am I allowed a phone call?" I ask.

He turns back to stare the stupidity of my question back at me.

"You could dial the number yourself," I say quickly. "It's just my friend, Kayla. She'll want to know that I'm okay, and…"

Bastien lets my words fade into a terrible silence. When he speaks, his words have a conciseness to them that cut into me. "What are you trying to do?"

"I'm just playing the game," I say. "Seeing what I can get out of this."

That's a lie—a stupid, pointless lie—but he doesn't need to know that.

"Playing the game," he repeats slowly. "Seeing what you can get."

Same words, but in a completely different tone. A dangerous one.

When he turns back to face me, his eyes are dark, his face expressionless. I'm more afraid of that blankness than all the scowls and glares in the world.

Because it's completely devoid of empathy. And when Bastien Nikolaev stops caring… something tells me there's no limit to what he'll do.

"You play with me," he says softly, crowding me into the corner, "and I'll play with you."

An involuntary whimper escapes my lips. Our eyes lock. Then his hand snakes up my skirt and palms the heat between my legs.

Sensation takes over as my knees turn to jelly. "Bastien…" I whimper.

"Shut up," he snarls softly. "It's my turn now."

I know what I should say. *Stop. No. Leave me alone.*

The problem is that "stop" is the last thing I want him to do. As his fingers dip past my panties and stroke against my clit, "stop" is no longer part of my vocabulary.

Not with the way he's touching me, the way he's feeling me…

Holy fucking God. Everything slackens, sharpens, into that one thing, that one press, pulse, pleasure. More of it and more of more of it, until I'm sinking onto his fingers and groaning softly under my breath.

He finds my clit with his thumb. Gentle pressure in slow circles, then faster and faster, until I come hard on his fingers. I bite the inside of my cheek so hard I taste blood.

For a few seconds afterward, his free hand cups the back of my head, almost tenderly. "That's a good girl," he murmurs in my ear. "Good girls come when they're told to."

One breath later, though, he's ripping himself away, grabbing me by the handcuffs and tugging me a few steps down the hallway.

"And good girls also remember who's in charge."

My feet don't seem to want to work. "B-Bastien?" I stutter.

He's talking like this was just a power play. The next step in the dance of submission and domination.

But there was something else. I wouldn't have given in so easily if it had just been that. I saw it in his eyes. There was something there. There was…

He yanks me up next to him. "Don't make me ask you again."

My anxious thoughts fall away in a slur of sadness. Once again, I am what I've been for ten years, what the Cubans made me—a doll on marionette strings.

He spins me around roughly and unlocks my handcuffs. I rub my wrists gingerly, wincing at the pain and the onrush of blood.

After he tucks the cuffs into his pocket, he reaches around me and opens the nearby door.

"This is your room," he says, shoving me inside.

He mutters something else I can't understand, then stalks out and slams the door shut behind him.

I stand there, listening to the twist of the door locking from the outside. And then I keep standing there. I stare at the door for much longer than necessary, at the small crack of light leaking out the bottom.

Then, sighing, I turn to face the interior darkness. I should've known that my one chance to escape would end like this—me stuck somewhere worse than ever.

Girls like me?

We don't get happy endings.

8

BASTIEN

"This should be good," Lukyan says as the SUV makes a smooth turn onto the highway. "An improvement from the other night's failure."

"It wasn't a failure," Evgeniy argues.

My teeth set together as my hand itches to go to my gun. In any situation, if there exist two different points of view, these goddamn brothers will find a way to assume opposite sides.

Leaving me in the middle. In this case, both literally and figuratively.

We're in the back, Lukyan on my left, Evgeniy on my right. I could've sat in the front and left our other man, Vitya, riding bitch like I am. But then the Limonov brothers would've been at each other's throats even worse.

Both literally and figuratively.

"It wasn't a success, either," Lukyan grumbles. His pale blue eyes are restless tonight. "It's not like we killed José himself, or anyone worthwhile. All we got was a bunch of old-timers, green new recruits, and…"

He trails off, careful to leave the rest unsaid.

... and some fiery dancer.

In the past few days since I brought Melissa to my house, he hasn't mentioned what happened.

How he almost shot her.

How he defied me.

He may be thick-headed sometimes, but he knows better than to bring that sore subject up. After all, the deal our driver is taking us to right this second is all thanks to me.

"It'll be nice to see your brother," Lukyan says to me. "Last time I saw him, he was a pudgy teenager, stuffing his face at Mom and Dad's wedding anniversary."

"Wasn't he banging one of the violinists?" Evgeniy recounts with half a smile.

I shrug. "Depends. Was she crazy?"

"I think she ended up bashing her violin against the wall and trying to beat a couple of people with her bow because someone made a critical comment about her playing or something."

"Then probably," I drawl. "Sounds like his type."

"But he ended up with someone else, didn't he?" Lukyan muses. "Another Nikolaev man who found his woman. He's engaged, no?"

"And she's not even crazy," I confirm. "Even my mother approves."

Lukyan whistles low. "We all know that isn't easy. Tetya Vanna is a tough customer. But have no fear, cousin—I'll get you hitched if that's what you want. You're interested in the best of the best? You just talk to me. I know every nice Russian girl in these parts... as well as the not-so-nice ones."

"Didn't one of your last girlfriends give you the clap?" Evgeniy asks the window he's looking out of.

"No," Lukyan growls. "But I'll clap you right in your smug fucking—"

I grab his hand as it jerks up.

His fist wilts almost immediately. He goes to angrily run a hand through his hair, then he scowls, as if disappointed to find himself not as wildly long-haired as he was in his teenage years.

"Sorry, Bastien. It was an escort who gave me it, not that it matters." He shoots a glare at Evgeniy, who is still peering out of the window.

"I'll only say this once," I tell the brothers. "Your fighting—it's a distraction. An unnecessary one. You cut it out, or we can solve this the old-fashioned way."

That shuts them up.

They know enough of our families' basic history to know what the "old-fashioned way" means. Two men in a ring with nothing but their bare hands. No one leaves until someone dies.

Not a solution I'd jump at, but a good one to mention casually all the same. Lukyan and Evgeniy should know better than to be squabbling like monkeys in a barrel.

"Understood," Lukyan says.

"Understood," Evgeniy says, but his back is still to me, his gaze out the window. Looking at what, who knows—the night out there is muggy and unremarkable, with a hint of rain yet to come, but more than enough mosquitoes to make up for it.

It's more like he's looking out there to avoid what's going on in here. Or rather, what's about to be going on as soon as we get where we're headed.

Stupid, though, for him to be tense now. We're going to a meeting with our own men, with little chance of danger.

Unless harmless little Evgeniy knows more than he's letting on...?

"Thanks for the offer, though," I tell Lukyan. I leave it at that, still eyeing the mountain range of tensions across Evgeniy's profile.

Betrayal from within has crossed my mind—of course it has. You have to be an idiot not to be suspicious of family just because they're family.

If I were José, I'd be looking for a crack in the Bratva, a rat in the ranks.

And Evgeniy shows all the signs of breaking.

"Suit yourself," Lukyan says. "Probably for the best. One look at your pretty eyes, and I'd lose half my regular girls."

I give him a distracted half-smile, still thinking.

In contrast to Evgeniy's moral disquiet, though, you couldn't get a more valuable or useful rat than Lukyan. Doesn't crack under pressure. Has the best idea of what's going on in Miami, having been his father's right-hand man.

Back in Boston, Gavriil and I strategized ourselves into a corner trying to figure out the rat in our ranks, while Patrick McNulty hit us with bold move after bold move.

I have no plans of making the same mistake.

First, deal with what I know. Hit the Cubans as much as I can. Act first—always. Throw your enemy onto the defense, on the run. Sow fear. Let the others stumble over conjecture and jump at shadows.

Everything else will sort itself out.

A few minutes later, we arrive.

"The Warehouse," they call it. What it really is is a piece-of-shit wreck so emptied out that even most urban explorers don't bother with it. Mired on a piece of land so out of the way—right beside a stinking dump—that even the owner, whoever they are, seems to have forgotten about it altogether.

I take one look at the filth-coated walls and grin.

Gavriil's gonna hate it.

By the looks of it, he's already beat us here. There's a nondescript car with its nose sticking out of the alleyway. I'm sure he's eager to handle business and get back to his empire, to his queen, back in Boston.

I text him as soon as we head out of the car to let him know that we're us and not unwanted visitors who should be welcomed with a hail of bullets. There is no such thing as being too careful.

"Welcome, welcome," my brother booms as we enter. The rusted metal doors scream in protest when we shove through and step onto the gouged cement floors. He spreads his arms to take in the whole place. "Thank you for your hospitality, for showing us the best Miami has to offer. Truly a palace fit for a king."

I laugh, getting a nose full of whatever shit-smelling dust is in here at the same time. "You want the Ritz next time, you just say the word."

"While you're at it, get me a platter with José Correa's head on it," he quips.

Now face to face, he throws his arms around me. I hug him back.

"That's the plan," I say as we separate. "How are the others?"

"You know Mother," Gavriil says with a warm smile on his harsh face. "She'd survive the apocalypse. She's already visited us in Boston half a dozen times. Has taken Hannah on a few shopping trips for the baby already—we don't know whether it's a girl or boy yet, but that hasn't stopped her from buying enough baby clothes to outfit half of the city's newborn population."

I smirk. "Your matching 'Proud Papa' and 'Proud Son' dino onesies are in the mail."

Gavriil gives me the finger and laughs. "Yeah, yeah. Get all the jokes out now so I don't have to hear them later."

"And Dmitry?" I ask.

"The regular old family man now," Gavriil says, his big, surprised smile indicating how unlikely that once was only a year or so back. "He's planning family dinners, working half-weeks to spend extra time with Shannon and little Katya. I can still hardly believe it."

"That makes two of us," I snort. Dmitry never seemed the settling down type. Neither did Gavriil, for that matter. I'm the only one who's stuck to my path.

"What about you?" he asks. "Still doing it solo?"

"I've barely unpacked my bags. Was I supposed to be betrothed by now?"

"Just be careful," Gavriil advises with that unflagging good humor he's had ever since he got engaged to Hannah. "It'll sneak up on you."

"I should introduce you," I say smoothly, changing the subject as I rotate to my cousins. "Or reintroduce you, rather. You remember Lukyan and Evgeniy."

Lukyan strides forward to pump Gavriil's hand eagerly. "I've heard great things about your time in charge, Gavriil. Taking down Patrick McNulty is no small feat."

"I had some help," he admits. "Bastien here played a big part in it. And the Irish bastard threatening my family, my fiancée? That fast-tracked me signing his death warrant. Not to mention what he did to our father."

Lukyan's gaze meets his with a glint of understanding. "I understand the feeling."

"I was sorry to hear about your loss," Gavriil says, somber now. "Uncle Maksi was a great man."

"The Cubans will pay," Lukyan answers. "José Correa most of all. Thank you for your condolences and your assistance."

"Happy to," Gavriil says with a nod. "We'll always be in debt to the Limonovs. Uncle Maksi was a great friend to our father."

He rotates to Evgeniy. "Good to see you, too, Evgeniy."

Strange how, with a body so huge and hulking, he still manages to blend into the background when he wants to.

They shake hands. Evgeniy mumbles, "Thanks for your support."

Gavriil gives a little shrug of his broad shoulders. "Truth be told, we don't need all these weapons at the moment—so we're happy to pass them on. Brothers share toys, isn't that right, Bastien?"

"Something like that," I mutter. "You sure you can manage without them?"

He waves a dismissive hand. "There's been barely any resistance since we put McNulty down and the last of the Irish scampered off. Although, we are keeping a lookout."

"Good," I say. "Should we get down to it?"

Gavriil chuckles and pats me on my shoulder. "Glad to see that you haven't lost your focus, *sobrat*. Just follow me to the back. We have our truck parked there. My men on the ground did an A+ job getting it here."

On our way there, Gavriil pauses, saying to me in an undertone, "No disrespect, brother, but if you need more help than we're offering, just say the word."

I eye him blankly.

He shrugs and sighs. "Well, I tried. Mother can't fault me for that."

"She put you up to this?" I demand.

Gavriil shrugs again. "She did and she didn't. It doesn't take a genius to see that things are a mess down here."

"That is a bigger understatement than you could possibly realize, brother."

"I could talk to Dmitry," Gavriil adds. "He's months away from the last time the cartel has given him any trouble. He'd be happy to—"

"That won't be necessary," I cut in.

Gavriil pauses. I pause, too. We're almost at the door. We need to hurry, but this conversation has to be finished first.

"I appreciate the offer," I rephrase. "But it won't be needed."

I've never been one to call a victory before it's settled, but the situation isn't desperate, either. More to the point, I don't want it to appear desperate. My cousins and the men know things are bad enough. Accepting backup from my brothers would write it in stone.

Not to mention that it would complicate things. I'm still getting a hold on my position and our maneuvers here in Miami. Importing new soldiers from Boston and New York would only give me more headaches to manage.

"You sure?"

"Things could come to that," I admit. "But until then..."

Gavriil nods as he continues through the door. "Understood. You gotta meet this new guy we just promoted, Ayton. He's a goddamn kill—"

A few steps outside, he falls silent and frowns. There's no one guarding his truck.

It couldn't be—

A bullet cuts through the silence.

"Back!" I roar into the night as I duck. Bullets slice right where I'd been standing seconds earlier.

Fucking hell. The Cubans got here fast.

Gavriil, my cousins, myself, and our men all race for the door, trading gunfire with the Cubans as we go. I see half a dozen silhouettes crouched in the shadows behind Gavriil's truck. Maybe more.

From inside the door, I see several familiar SUVs come roaring up. That's the backup I was counting on.

Granted, I didn't expect things to happen at the back, but luckily, my men were ready for whatever.

Over the next few minutes, my men decimate the Cubans who linger and run down any others who try to make a run for it. Gavriil, my cousins, and I provide cover fire from our vantage point.

Once the last Cuban has fallen to the ground, letting loose a string of insults in grunted Spanish as he dies, Lukyan turns to me with shining eyes. "Now, *that's* the motherfucking Nikolaev brothers I've heard about!"

Gavriil chuckles. "Don't believe everything you hear."

"We were well-prepared," I say. "But we also got lucky. After their last successful hit and our botched hit on El Palacio, the Cubans underestimated us. Unlikely that they'll make that mistake again."

Lukyan looks pleased anyway. The man feeds off bloodlust. Evgeniy, on the other hand, looks worse off than some of the corpses.

Afterwards, Gavriil and I stand off to the side, discussing things.

"The Cubans are getting aggressive," Gavriil says dubiously, doing a count of the bodies.

"Good thing I was prepared," I say. "With the way these hits have been coming, I can't say I'm surprised."

"They're doing things how you would," he agrees. "Hit fast and hit hard."

Our eyes meet.

"They shouldn't have been able to find us here," I say quietly. "Unless they were watching us, someone monitoring our actions."

"A possibility," Gavriil agrees, his dark eyes sliding my way, murky with agreement and also something else, something more insidious. "Have you considered the other one?"

"Of course."

"I know last time we ran after our own asses trying to find the spy," he admits. "But it never hurts to be on your guard."

"Most of these men are new to me," I sigh. "If I have to be suspicious of any, I'd have to be suspicious of all."

"Just keep your eye out. Make sure there are no Stacys lurking about." Seeing my face darken, his brows jump again. "Oh?"

"It's… nothing."

He shrugs. "I'm not trying to interfere. This is your territory now."

"True."

He sighs. "Okay, maybe I'm just…"

"Nosy," I finish for him.

He chuckles. "Nosy, helpful, call it what you want."

"There was a hostage recently. A girl we took from the club we burned down," I admit. "But she's locked up in my basement. There's no way she could've known about our plan, about any of this."

"A hostage, eh?" Gavriil says with a smile that's annoyingly aware. "Female? Pretty?"

"Doesn't matter," I snap. "I handled it. It's a non-issue."

"Yeah, yeah." His smile grows. "Forgive me if I have my doubts."

I look at him flatly. This conversation is not moving into productive territory.

"Be careful, brother," he jokes, wiggling his eyebrows suggestively. "You might not be as stone-hearted as you think. Hell, stranger things have happened. Like Dmitry falling for his forced bride, me falling for my employee..."

"Lukyan wasn't happy," I say instead of taking his bait. "With me saving her. But I had to. It was our way."

Gavriil nods in understanding. "Father would be proud. As for Lukyan, though... has he been moody lately?"

I shrug. "Hard to say. I'm keeping an eye out, though."

"You do that," Gavriil says quietly.

He doesn't have to say what's at stake if this fails and we let it go too far.

That's the thing about family empires: strengthen one and you strengthen all. Topple one... and the others start to shake.

If I fail here, the ripple effect could destroy everything the Nikolaevs have fought for and conquered over the decades. We could lose everything we hold dear.

Our empire.

Our family.

Our lives.

9

MELISSA

I glare at the cement walls. How is it that I escape one crappy, monotonous existence for another crappier, even more monotonous one?

At least back at the club, I could talk to people. I had Kayla. Here, on the other hand, I have…

I do an unimpressed inventory of the room, even though I already know what I'll find.

Rusty toilet and decrepit sink in an unfinished, doorless bathroom? Check.

Cracker-thin bare mattress with one suspiciously stained pillow? Check.

A leak in the corner, an alarmingly large spider setting up shop way too close to the bed, and not a single goddamn thing to stave off the incoming insanity? Check, check, and check.

I rub my eyes and stretch, trying to think. How many days has it been? Three or four, give or take? At first, I just slept a bunch, so it's hard to tell for sure. The lack of any windows doesn't help.

Not that it matters. The Cubans aren't about to send a search and rescue party out for me, even if they did know where I was imprisoned.

A low chuckle rolls out of my throat. Yep, I can just about see it now: José, his boyish face with those bulgy eyes bulged even more with panic, saying, *God, no, we can't let them have our Melissa! The way she cleaned the floors at the end of the night...! How she half-heartedly shook those hips to the music...!*

My chuckle turns into a sigh.

Yeah. Not happening.

Another song comes into my head, an old lullaby Mama used to hum to me at night. I start singing it. It makes me feel a bit better, even if I'm hungry and there's no way of knowing when or if Bastien will be coming down with a meal.

Judging by my rumbling stomach, it shouldn't be long now. He's been fairly regular thus far.

"Mama," I sigh to the empty room as I sink onto the bed, "what do you think of all this?"

"My poor girl," I almost hear her sigh. A guilty tremor goes through me. After all this time and no pictures, I can hardly remember her face. But her voice... that's ingrained in me. "My poor, poor girl."

"Should I try escaping?"

"You know I can't tell you that." Her voice is warm and loving and so sad that it makes me tear up.

"If I messed up, maybe I could join you," I murmur aloud.

"Don't be ridiculous," she scolds. "You know I wouldn't want that."

"No," I say. "No, I *don't* know, actually. I don't know what you want because you're dead and I'm just talking to a figment of my own imagination right now."

Silence. No more Mama.

So much for a heartwarming moment with my mother's memory. Maybe if I try...

"Hey, Kayla," I say, switching over. "Miss me yet?"

"Like a fat kid loves cake. Not quite the exact right expression, but you get the point."

"Bring those jokes to work," I laugh. "The clientele will love you."

"Ugh. Work. What a shitshow. Is El Palacio the worst place on Earth to work at?" Mind-Kayla asks.

"Without a doubt," I say. "But I guess they have no choice but to give you some days off now, huh?"

"Pfft," Kayla says, voice laced with derision. I can see her in my head: dark auburn hair, honey-brown eyes with whatever bright lipstick or nail polish she's going with for today. "Who do you think's doing most of the clean-up?"

"That sounds like our José," I say sadly. "Everyone you've ever known or loved is dead with a Russian bullet in their forehead? Sucks. See you on Monday."

He's never been one to take it easy on anyone.

There's a story some of the younger asshole guys like to laugh about. How, when one of their slaves, Yvonne—seventy-something and using a cane—had to go to the hospital for pneumonia, José put her right back to work mopping floors the same day she was released. She was dead within a week.

"Anyway, you take care of yourself, babe," Kayla continues. "You hear?"

"Yeah, yeah," I say. "You, too."

The conversation should end there, but I'm lonely and bored, so I add, "I'll see you again someday... okay?"

Silence.

I sigh. Even Imaginary Kayla is done with me.

I grab my black pleather purse and dump out my carefully packed-away belongings. With everything I have left to my name scattered on the bed, I run through a lame rollcall that confirms their uselessness.

Bastien didn't leave me with my phone, of course. Just four Super Tampax Tampons, a half-used lipstick in a mauve-brown color I don't even like, seven cents in pennies from the early 2000s, some stretched-out hair elastics and a rusting bobby pin...

Hold up.

Bobby pins. Haven't I seen in some movie or read in some book about how some character used bobby pins to pick the lock?

Because Hollywood movies and fictional books always play things out realistically, I snark to myself.

My fingers close around the peeling black metal. What do I have to lose?

I pause, listening for Bastien. Nothing.

I head to the foot of the stairs that lead up to the ground floor, pausing again. Still nothing.

I'm pretty sure he's not even in the house. Not that he's a stomper. He moves pretty damn quiet for such a big man, actually. The droning of his air conditioning isn't helping me know for sure whether or not he's here, though.

I climb up a couple stairs, then pause. A few more, then I pause again.

And still, there's nothing.

Is this the window of opportunity I've spent ten years waiting for?

I peer at the lock and the hole. It looks pickable, but then again, what the hell do I know? "Not much" is the short answer. Not enough to know whether this will work, whether I'm signing my own death warrant, whether he's waiting on the other side to see if I'm really stupid enough to try escaping.

"Only one way to find out," I mumble to myself.

I shove the bobby pin in. I jiggle it and… nothing. No *"you got it!"* click, no chorus of angels praising my ingenuity and derring-do.

I exhale, jiggle the handle more furiously, then wait.

Well, if Bastien is in fact in the house, me being really loud and obvious will probably bring him right here.

But I don't hear anything, so…

I glare at the bobby pin. Not that I expected it to work right away, but… shoot, I don't know. Google would really come in handy right now.

"Take two," I mutter to myself, grabbing the bobby pin and getting back to work.

At first, as I pull it out and try shoving it in again, I don't feel anything other than a hole that doesn't fit. But then, gradually, I feel different indentations in the lock, almost like…

Oh my God, I'm getting it. *I'm actually getting it!*

Just then, though, I hear something that makes my heart drop to the bottom of my gut.

Footsteps.

Coming right this way.

Oh, shit—I rip the bobby pin out. Or at least, I try to. Which of course is when it decides to jam.

Shit, shit, shit!

The thing won't come out no matter how hard I tug on it. I give it one final desperate rip—only to have it crack in two. Leaving half the evidence in the most obvious place possible.

Fuck.

My.

Life.

But there's no time to bemoan my shitty luck. I rush downstairs and have just plopped myself on the bed when the door creaks open.

Well, at least I didn't completely ruin the lock?

It's Bastien, of course. He's advancing with a plate full of pasta that he hands me without a word. Same as usual. Whatever happened between us the night we met, Bastien seems determined to forget it. He's stuck resolutely to his plan of leaving me here to rot.

I fidget, trying not to look quite so *Yeah I've been trying to escape via bobby pin, but it's no big deal.*

"Hey," I say suddenly. "Can I shower? It's been days."

"No."

"Maybe another day soon, then?"

He pauses, but doesn't answer.

"Look, I know you don't want to talk to me, but would it kill you to say a few words? I'm kind of going crazy down here."

Still no answer. I might as well be talking to an Imaginary Bastien, just like my Mom and Kayla. But shit, they talked more than he does—and they are literally not real.

"There's a sink down here," he says with a dismissive wave in its direction.

"Please," I beg. "Unless you're afraid that scary little me can overpower you with a showerhead. Or did some mean boys in high school terrorize you with wet towel flicks, and now you're afraid I'll use that as a weapon?"

He rolls his eyes and starts to turn for the stairs again.

"Wait!" I cry out. "If you help me out, I could help you out."

God, I sound like some gangster in a Hallmark made-for-TV movie.

"Meaning...?" He's swiveled back around now and is regarding me with those flat, dark eyes.

"Meaning the Cubans held me captive in their club for ten years," I tell him. "There's no way I didn't pick stuff up along the way."

His face and eyes are as hard as before I spoke. "I doubt they discussed plans in the middle of a club right in front of a dancer."

"I never said they did," I retort. "But I do know how they live, how they act."

Bastien studies me, then gestures to my plate. "Eat."

He stands there, watching me. For some reason, I find that irritating.

I can't pretend I'm not starving, though. And it wouldn't do much good if I did. So I keep shoveling food down my throat like the Cookie Monster.

I tell myself that I don't care what this asshole thinks of me or my eating habits. But as I wolf down these bare, buttered noodles and he stands there watching me, there's a weird tension between us.

As if last time, when Bastien touched me and made me come on his fingers like some cheap slut, wasn't even the beginning of it.

"Is there a reason you have to watch me eat?" I ask between mouthfuls.

His gaze doesn't waver. He just shrugs.

"Suit yourself," I say with my own shrug.

"I always do."

Now, it's my turn to roll my eyes. "There," I say, showing him my empty plate once I'm done. I believe it's been less than forty-five seconds since bite number one went down the hatch. "Now, can I shower?"

He takes a good few seconds before answering. "Fine. Leave your plate here and follow me."

I do so, but on the stairs, he pauses. His grip closes on my arm. It isn't a violent or painful grip. Just a firm one. The one you'd give to your favorite dog who likes to misbehave. A grip of ownership.

An odd tingle goes through me.

Then he lets go with a sigh and opens the door at the top of the landing.

I step through. Seeing the rest of the house in the light of day is a worthwhile experience in itself. There's been a lot more care taken in this part than in the basement, that's for sure.

There is a minimalist style here, but the few furniture pieces that are here have a sort of vintage charm to them: intricately carved mahogany legs, a familiar painting on the walls. I recognize some of them from...

God, was it really ten whole years ago since Mom and I hit up the local library, sitting in their creased leather seats to flip through an equally creased art book?

"Is that Toulouse-Lautrec?" I ask, as we move on to the wooden stairs, my gaze lingering on a colorful oil.

"You know him?" He sounds surprised.

"My parents taught me," I say quietly. "They loved art. Every weekend, we'd check out another museum on the free evenings. We'd hit up the library to look at art books. My mom even used to do these beautiful paintings…" I trail off.

What the hell am I doing, telling Bastien all this? He certainly doesn't give a shit, and it doesn't benefit me, either.

What it is is pitiful. He shows me the smallest morsel of kindness, and I go blabbing my life story to him.

Whatever he thinks of that, it doesn't show. He tugs me further up the stairs without another word or any sign that anything happened.

Mental note: *he doesn't care, Melissa.*

The bathroom is nice. Blue porcelain tile walls and floor with a pearly white sink and shower. Clean, brightly lit, a stark contrast to the prison cell downstairs.

I stand there for a few seconds before I realize what's wrong: Bastien's closed the door behind us. He's standing inside as if he belongs here.

"Welp," I say, glancing at Bastien nervously, "I think I can take it from here."

He doesn't say anything. Just looks at me. God, the whole mysterious-and-silent act is getting old.

I point to the shower. "I don't need you to show me how it works. I can handle it myself."

"I'm not here to show you how the shower works."

I gaze at him. "Then what are you here for?"

He leans against the doorframe. "To make sure you don't do anything crazy."

"Like what?" I ask, incredulous. "Hang myself off the shower rod? Jump out the window?"

I glance out the window and see the three-story vertical drop. Even if I could wriggle through the small opening, there's no way I'd survive the plunge, and I'm not desperate enough to try just yet.

Bastien doesn't seem to care to argue, though. He just stands there and doesn't say a word.

Jesus, he's really going to just sit there, while I...

I swallow, as that same stupid tremble goes through me. Yeah, maybe his tone was all business, but after what happened between us...

I turn away from him to get my breath under control. *Just business,* I repeat to myself in my head. *That's all this is.*

But pulling off my sequined bra in front of him is not "just business," no matter how many times I repeat that mantra to myself.

Even if my back is to him as I do, I can feel his eyes, resting on me, drinking me in. The contours of my spine, my hips.

And then I'm pulling off my skirt and my panties and I can feel his gaze burning into me, as intimate as a touch.

My skin crawls with the realization that all he'd need to do is say a single word for me to be his again. One word—that's all it would take.

Come...

I hurry into the shower, slam the glass door behind me, and crank on the tap. I exhale in thankfulness as the hot water cascades over my shoulder, washing away days' worth of blood and sweat and grime and tears.

God, I needed this.

Thankfully, the glass is at least partially clouded, blurring out just above my tits to my upper leg. By now, he's probably looked away, gotten bored and...

I chance a glance and freeze.

Our eyes meet, and my hypothesis is proven wrong.

No, Bastien Nikolaev hasn't gotten bored yet. Far from it. That look, the fiery want in those eyes...

I rip my gaze away.

If I let myself give into the heat between my legs that has nothing to do with the steaming shower, there's no telling what could happen.

Being near Bastien is its own brand of danger. One that has nothing to do with guns or even his fists. More like what's behind his zipper...

I grab the shampoo bottle angrily. But when I squirt some into my hand, a familiar scent sends me reeling.

It's *guava*.

And just like that, everything shifts. For the first time, I see it—I'm not as helpless or as powerless as I thought I was just a second ago.

Because I have more of a foothold on Mr. Nikolaev than he's letting on.

"Do you like how I smell, Bastien?" I ask innocently.

The confidence of the discovery is fading quickly, though. I could be wrong. And even if he did buy this on purpose, so what if he bought the same scent as José forced us to wear in the club?

It could be a coincidence, it could be...

"You must be done," he announces. He pushes himself off the wall and walks over to the glass partition.

My heart does a jump, half-terrified, half-excited. I can almost see it now: him shoving open the door, grabbing me. Pinning me up against the wet tile as the water poured over us.

How my body would betray me before my mind could even start to think of how to resist.

He's just a couple of inches away from me. "Kissing distance," as Kayla used to call it. Only a thin pane of glass between us.

"Well?"

"No!" I squeak.

"If you've got enough time to be making jokes, seems like you must be finished," he continues.

"No, I'm sorry—I'll concentrate," I say. I pour out some of the shampoo and massage it into my scalp. "I am—see?"

"Good." That one little word resounds in me, weirdly satisfying. It's a vaguely familiar feeling, too. Like a faint echo of what he said to me in the hallway the night he brought me here.

That's a good girl. Good girls come when they're told to.

For the rest of the shower, I'm caught in an unbearable limbo. I try to pretend he isn't there, standing only a few inches away, watching my every move.

But I can't.

I can't shake the feeling that he doesn't so much as glance away from me, doesn't even dare blink. That the only reason for his attention is the kind of lust that ruins people. The kind that's ruining me.

And yet at the same time, I can't bring myself to sneak a glance. He'd see it and know what it means—that he's already won.

So instead, I enjoy the hot beads of water rolling over my skin as much as I can, singing a bit, rubbing soap and a loofah over myself, before finishing up with some conditioner. It's new, too, and also guava-scented.

At the end, I turn off the shower.

"Towel?" I ask.

Bastien tosses a white one over the top of the stall. Like the shampoo and conditioner, it's brand new. I wrap myself in thick Egyptian cotton, then step out of the shower. I avoid his eyes, even though I can feel them on me still.

"Thanks."

He doesn't answer. Which is good. Maybe.

It's easier this way.

Although, I can't help thinking, as he grabs my hand and heads us back to the basement, that I've been stripping for years…

And never before have I felt as exposed as I do when I'm around Bastien Nikolaev.

10

BASTIEN

"Te regalo mi cintura... Y mis labios para cuando quieras besar..."

My teeth clang on the fork in my mouth. Not this again.

Wasn't how she teased me during that shower a few days ago fucking enough? Stripping like she was enjoying it, nice and slow, then singing and rubbing herself all over, even slower, her hair slick and gaze coy, like it was all part of the show...

The first time I jerked off, mere minutes after I locked her back downstairs, I figured that would get it out of my system.

It didn't.

Now, thanks to the vent on the floor that leads down to the basement, her singing wanders up here whenever I least expect it.

I let the fork clatter onto the plate. It's still half full, but I've suddenly lost my appetite. The chair screeches backwards over the kitchen tiles as I stand up.

Might as well get this shit over with.

I storm upstairs into my bedroom, slam the door behind me, sling myself on my bed. Here, I'm far enough away that her voice is at least out of my ears.

Out of my mind, though?

Not a chance.

I can see it now, how that other time in the shower should've ended. Was so close to ending. When I was standing there at the shower door, inches away, separated by mere glass and the last sliver of my self-control...

Towering over her like that, I could see down to what the blurred glass obscured from across the room. Those perfect, pert tits, those generous hips, *fuck*...

I free my cock from my zipper and start stroking.

Yeah, just one push open of that door, and she would've been mine. Would her kiss have that bratty insolence that fires me up? Would she taste like defiance?

The scene keeps unfolding in my head the way it should have gone. I'd press her back into the tiles and hold her there with both palms to get a better look at her.

She'd squirm, wanting more. I'd laugh in her face.

Then I'd lean in to devour her. Lips twisting, tongues clashing. She'd grab my cock, still covered by jeans. I'd grab her pussy, bare and wet.

She'd wilt onto me, whimpering. The last of her fight snuffed out.

One look, one parting of her lips, that's it. It would be obvious. *She needed this.*

I'd push her away so I could rip off my clothes. Then I'd spin her around and shove her back into the wall, her face pressing into the porcelain tiles.

She'd already be moaning my name into them. "Bastien..." Saying it not with the fear and respect I'm accustomed to, but with something else. A kind of familiarity that makes my skin flush with anger and lust.

It pisses me off when she says my name like we're something to each other.

It also gets me rock fucking hard.

I'd press my body against hers so she can feel my hulking erection against her ass and snarl in her ear, "Call me Mr. Nikolaev."

Then, before she can even formulate another bratty response, I'd shove my throbbing cock into her wetness.

She'd cry out, I'm sure. She's never had someone as big as me before. But as I filled her, as she adjusted to me, as she melted around me, she'd know—she'll never settle for anyone else again.

She'd be spasming already, just a few strokes into it. Her whole body trembling, teetering near the edge.

So I'd help her over it.

I'd pick her up, wrap her legs around my waist with my hands under that ass, and fuck her the way the saucy little minx deserves. Move her on me and off me. In and out, fast and faster.

She'd cry out and moan, words slurring, louder than ever. Her body would be shaking so hard I would have to hold her even tighter so she didn't fall to pieces.

And as she came, my name—my *proper* name—would hum on her lips like a prayer.

Mr. Nikolaev...

Mr. Nikolaev...

Mr. Nikolaev...

That's when I'd lose it. I'd erupt into her with everything I had.

And she'd take it all.

Because that's what good girls do.

As I lose it in my fantasy, I do the same in reality, coming so hard I can barely breathe. Afterwards, I lay there, glaring at the ceiling.

Another night of this. Another useless waste.

And sure enough, as my breath eases back to its normal control, as my heartbeat calms... my cock twitches back to life, as strong and stubborn as ever.

For fuck's sake. I might as well not have jerked off at all.

My phone goes off on the nightstand. I reach over and grab it. It's Lukyan.

"Just checking in," he says when I answer. "How goes it?"

"Uneventful." I'm in no mood to make small talk or do anything other than be alone. "We'll talk tomorrow."

"Prisoner giving you any trouble?" he says, careful to keep his voice light.

"Why?" I ask, keeping mine just as light. As light as a finger seconds away from the trigger. "Getting bored with your normal duties and want to keep watch?"

"Don't tempt me," Lukyan says with a chuckle. "Watching a girl that fine must have its perks."

Watch your tongue, I almost growl out before I bite my tongue.

I'm surprised at the anger spiking through me. As if I have any real sort of claim over the woman locked up in my basement. Or care what happens to her.

"Don't worry about me," I say. I grab a gun from the drawer and start to load and unload it, over and over again. It's a sort of meditation for me. "I never let pleasure get in the way of business."

"If you say so," Lukyan says. "You're really just keeping her locked up down there? No food, no water?"

"I provide meals."

I don't mention how I've been hanging around the basement while she takes her sweet time eating them—solely to make sure she doesn't try anything. Broken plates and cutlery can make usable weapons if desperation and stealth are combined.

I don't tell him how I've caught myself lingering just above the vent in the hallway to listen to her sing.

That shit is on a need-to-know basis. And he sure as fuck doesn't need to know.

Lukyan whistles. "Have to say, cousin, you've been true to form. Better than. If only more of our men were like you. I'd trade that useless shit Evgeniy in a second for half of—"

"Don't be too hard on him," I say. "He can't help what he is."

"There's always a choice," Lukyan argues. "I had to choose, once. We all did. Papa let us decide, though he did pressure us. Thing is, Evgeniy's weak. Always has been, always will be. Back then, he was too weak to stand up for himself, too weak to do anything in his own right. My brother's problem is that he's made his choice—but he's been trying to back out of it ever since."

"Wartime isn't easy," I say simply.

I'm half-disgusted with myself. Who the hell knows why I'm defending Evgeniy? Other than the fact that it's pointless to curse his failings. You use the tools you're given, no more, no less.

"That, it's not," Lukyan agrees soberly. "I still can't believe he's gone, you know. My father. You won't believe how many times I'm about to call him up before I remember. Losing a father is…"

He trails off as it suddenly occurs to him that he's not the only one who's lost a father in recent times.

"Sorry," he says gruffly. "Forget I said anything."

"Uncle Maksi was a great man," I say. "And he will be avenged. But we can't rush it."

"I know," Lukyan says. "I just—I can't get it out of my head, how he looked when we found him: ashen-faced, like they'd somehow sucked all the life and happiness out of him right before they put that bullet in him. And that fucking Cuban cigar in his mouth. I want to put a thousand of those cigars out on José Correa's skin. I want to watch him burn and suffer and scream."

"You'll get that chance. In time."

"I know. All this is just to say that I know my head isn't screwed on right at the moment. I screwed up before, back at El Palacio. Took things too far."

"It's okay," I tell him. "Forgiven."

"It's not," he growls. "Screw this up, and it won't be just my father I've lost; it'll be everything he held dear. This entire empire he built."

"It's easy to get distracted," I say. "It's what the Cubans are expecting. It's why we have to keep vigilant."

"If my ass gets out of line again, you tell me," Lukyan says. "I need it. God knows Evgeniy doesn't do it."

"I will. Rest assured."

"Good. And if you change your mind about those girls—just let me know," Lukyan adds cheekily. "There's this one chick, let me tell you: white-blonde hair all the way to her ass, seems like an innocent little sweetheart, but in bed… damn. And there are these ginger twins… I swear, you wouldn't believe this shit unless you saw it yourself." He sighs, caught up in his own narrative. "Oh, and also, this waitress, huge tits and a mouth like a goddamn vac—"

"I'll be fine," I cut him off. "Keep them to yourself."

"As you wish, captain," Lukyan answers. "Only all work and no play can make a man—"

"I know what it makes me."

I don't add the rest. That it's a sort of edge I have, this keeping on the knife-edge of things. The farther I dedicate myself to my work, this empire-building, the farther I go.

Too many people allow themselves too many diversions. Little by little, they give their power away, one micro-transaction at a time. It makes them weak.

Not me.

"Good of you to check in, Lukyan," I tell him. "The hit on Thursday will be good."

"I'm looking forward to it," he says.

I hang up, then pause, frowning. Takes a few seconds for it to sink in why.

Then "… *Y mis labios para cuando quieras besar…*" echoes in from the vent.

I stand there, my hands fisting then unfisting, over and over again. My gaze flickers outside to the murky, starless sky and empty street.

I should go for a run. Clear my head. Instead, I do what I shouldn't do.

I go downstairs.

Next thing I know, I'm a step away from the door, stopped to listen. The problem is, the singing stops a moment later.

"Like what you hear, Bastien?" she calls in a sassy voice.

Fuck. This was a bad idea. I scowl, turning away.

"Or did you have a request?" I can hear her moving up the stairs towards me. "C'mon, I know you're there."

"Checking up on you," I say briskly. "Making sure you aren't planning something stupid."

"Yeah, because you always can tell a girl's about to escape when she starts singing, right?"

Not seeing her makes this easier. Although the image of Melissa dancing in my mind's eye is doing me no favors.

I turn to leave when she adds, "Just admit it: you like hearing my voice. Why not sing along? I might know a Russian song or two…"

I bite the inside of my cheek until I taste blood. "Go back downstairs. I have work to do."

She makes a skeptical noise. "Why check up on me at all, if you're so busy?"

"This conversation is over."

"No, you know what I think?" she says. She's at the door now. I can see her shadow blocking the thin line of light at the bottom. "I think you've been thinking about me more than you want to."

"Are you trying to lose shower privileges?" I ask.

"I had them?" When I don't answer, she continues, "I saw how you looked at me."

Turn away, Bastien. Leave. I don't take the bait—I say nothing.

But I don't move, either.

"I bet you've been thinking about me. About doing things to me," she says.

"The thought of killing you to spare myself the trouble has crossed my mind," I drawl.

"Bastien!" she exclaims in horror.

"What did we say about my name?"

Silence. My hands relax. Good. Now, I can turn away and get back to...

"You didn't mean it," she says with a quiet forcefulness.

"I assure you I did."

"Bastien," she says quietly. "I mean, Mr. Nikolaev..."

"Just go back downstairs."

"What difference does it make to you?" she demands. "I'm stuck down here either way."

"Your voice is distracting," I say.

"Distracting in a good way, or a bad way?" She's back with that alluring voice again, that voice that knows more than it should. "Just admit it: you've been thinking about me, because that's what you want."

"Or maybe you've been thinking about me—because that's what *you* want."

"Maybe. But it's different. You're on that side of the door, and I'm on this side. And besides—aren't you the kind of man who *takes* what he wants?"

I'm not too stupid to recognize a dare. A challenge.

Nor am I so stupid as to take her up on it.

I turn away, force myself to the front door. But it's not far enough.

"Leaving so soon?" she murmurs.

"This is a waste of time."

"Lucky for you, baby, I've got all the time in the world," she says with a bitter laugh.

I open the front door of the house. The night air is cool and quiet enough to suit me. A run really would do me good. Drive the blood from my brain and my cock to my legs. Convert useless thought into action.

"Wait!" she calls through the locked door. "Don't go."

"Why not?"

"Because… I don't want you to."

Her voice is choked with—fuck, I don't know, but with something. The same something that's weighing down on my chest right now, perhaps. All I can hear is the sound of my labored breathing.

Then…

"Open the door, Bastien. Enough games."

She's right. Enough games. This ends tonight how it should've started.

Me and her.

Right here.

Right now.

11

MELISSA

The door rips open, and all I can think is, *What have I done?*

He towers over me even more than usual since he's on the highest step of the staircase. Those dark, gorgeous eyes capture all the light in the room.

I used to be afraid he'd kill me.

Now, I'm afraid of all the other things he might do instead.

His voice is cool and expressionless as he devours me with his gaze. "Well?" he rumbles.

I swallow hard, at a complete loss for words. When he was on the other side, this seemed like a good idea.

Now?

Not so much.

"You wanted the door open, Melissa," he adds. "You wanted me here. Well, you have me. What comes next in your bold little plan?"

Say something, dammit. Say anything.

But my tongue is desert-dry and if I ever knew how to speak English, I seem to have forgotten it the second he turned the doorknob.

A tense, crackling moment passes back and forth between us. It could turn into something else if I let it. If I pushed it. All I have to do is say something…

"I…"

But the words die on my lips.

Bastien scowls in disgust. I ruined it. He turns away, about to leave again.

My mind is in overdrive, a thousand voices screeching over one another. *Bastien's a man, and by definition, that makes him bad. Every man I've ever met has been a monster in one way or another. What makes him different?*

The answer to that question is obvious.

Everything.

"Wait!" I burst out as he opens the door.

Bastien pauses. "For?"

"This." And then I'm moving, my hands are moving, turning his face so I can find his mouth with a kiss, all before my brain can even begin to process what's happening.

Hello there.

Ohhh… fuck.

I'm in for it now.

He growls right into my kiss, then pivots to press me into the wall that runs along the stairs. I feel tiny and fragile in his arms. He could break me with just the slightest effort.

Maybe that's what I want.

His musk overpowers me. All I can see or taste or smell is *him.* His chest is impossibly strong, and below, I can feel how hard and massive he is.

Something murmurs in me, something long forgotten: *Be careful.*

Of what?

Of the way he kisses me like he knows me already?

Of the way he knows what I want without ever needing to ask?

Or maybe I should be careful of how my pussy's already grinding against his hardened cock, separated by only a few layers that already seem insubstantial.

The kiss builds. He pulls away just to make me gasp, to tease me, to play with me.

I shouldn't give into those silly little power games. But I'm operating on autopilot now. I can't be careful. How could I be, when all the blood in my body is concentrated in my lips and throbbing between my legs? There's none left for thinking.

I pull away just far enough to whisper, "Are you going to hurt me, Bastien?"

His answer is immediate. "Only if you beg for it."

Then he spins me around and shoves me face-first against the brick wall. It's not gentle or romantic—it's fucking feral, two animals locked in heat.

He rips up the hem of my skirt, slides his hand around my hip, and delves underneath my panties to find my pussy.

"You're already wet for me, princess," he snarls right in my ear. I can feel his breath on my cheek, hot and fragrant. "How long have you been dreaming of this?"

All I can do is whimper into the brick.

He parts my folds and slides one thick finger inside of me. His thumb flickers over my clit and I almost come right then and there.

I'm trapped between a rock and a hard place—more or less literally— and I'm about to come, moaning like a porn star, within three seconds of being touched.

So much for keeping it together.

But how can I? It feels like I was made to shatter in this way.

It builds in me, hot and raging and wild, from my center, up and up, until my whole body is shaking with it and my orgasm crashes through me and I'm crying out and he's holding me and it's better than anything I've ever felt.

My legs give out, but Bastien doesn't let me fall. He presses his hips into mine to keep me upright. His dick is hard and insistent in his pants. I can feel it, like a threat I know he will make good on.

The heat between my legs slackens for maybe the length of a breath before it rekindles and the orgasm fades. What's left behind is raw need.

I spin back around. My hands go to his belt. His hand goes to the back of my head.

But just as I'm about to rip his jeans down, his hand pulls away. He takes a step back and turns to face the door.

I almost scream in frustration like a bratty little girl. Step back, turn away, slow down, stop—*now?* For the love of God, *why?*

He's breathing hard before me, back still turned. His shoulders rise and fall with every labored inhale and exhale. But less and less each time. Until he's once again what he's always been—an icy statue of perfect control.

But the question remains: *Why?* Because letting myself spin out of control just now was the best thing I've ever felt.

My forehead muscles clench with frustration. I force myself to take a breath.

"Where did you learn to sing?" he asks quietly.

I almost laugh out loud. Of all the million things I would've guessed he'd say next, that had to be near the bottom of the list.

"Why? Want lessons?"

He still isn't facing me and doesn't respond. Guess the time for teasing is over.

I sink to a seat on the step. "My mother was a singer at a Cuban club," I say, more subdued.

A smile touches my lips as I recall it. Just like that, I'm back there. Strings of fire-colored paper lanterns swinging to the salsa beat, chalk-decorated cement floor, and it seemed like they all wore the same lazy smile back then. The whole colorfully Cuban crowd like a big, rowdy family.

"My parents would take me along with them to the club. Couldn't afford a babysitter. I'd sing along, I guess, and one time, my mama realized it didn't sound half-bad. When I got a bit older, we sang together. There was this nice old man, he must've been a hundred or something, he'd bring these orange carnations and throw them to our feet at the end of our last song of the night. It was nice for a while."

"For a while," Bastien says. Catching on the only three words there that really matter.

At some point while I was talking, he turned. Now, he's gazing down at me with an impenetrable darkness in his eyes.

"Why?" I snap, suddenly irritable. "Do I look like someone who had a pampered life growing up? Not everyone is born into mob royalty, you know. Do you think I even know what the fuck a silver spoon tastes like?"

"No," he says simply. "I don't."

He doesn't blink or look away—but I do. I don't want him to see the vulnerability in my eyes. Men like him can only do one thing when they see that: exploit it.

The silence throbs around us. "What about you?" I say, if only to say something. To fill the silence.

I never much minded it before I met Bastien Nikolaev. Maybe because the silence around him isn't just empty space. It's a message in and of itself. Full of hidden meanings.

"In some ways, my brothers and I led very pampered lives," he admits. "My parents were loving, generous, wealthy." His face darkens. "In other ways… we were not so lucky."

It hits me then—a memory, a little scrap of gossip finally weaving itself into place so I can make sense of it. Before I started hearing about what bigshots the infamous Nikolaev brothers were becoming, I heard about a hit. A big one.

"Papa Nikolaev took the plunge," I remember one of El Palacio's regulars saying. The meaning was clear: Andrushka Nikolaev was dead.

He'd always been a distant, shadowy figure. Like the boogeyman. Far away in New York, but even down here, his power could be felt.

To hear he was dead, though, made him suddenly feel human to me. The boogeyman can't die.

But Andrushka Nikolaev could.

So maybe Bastien does know what it's like. How real pain can cut you up, hollow you out.

"Do you miss him?"

Bastien's eyes almost meet mine. His lips almost part. He almost says something. Maybe even something honest.

Key word: almost.

Instead, though, he turns his back on me. The meaning of the gesture is clear: *Playtime is over.* Which makes sense, of course. That's all I am to him. To every man on this planet.

A stupid little plaything.

"It's okay if you do, you know. I miss my parents. The Cubans, they aren't exactly known for their mercy. When they found out my dad was an informer, they killed him. Took Mama and me as prisoners."

"Is that so?" His voice is so distant that it almost hurts me.

I tug my panties back into place, yank my skirt back down over my ass, and rise slowly to my feet. "Not that that's any of your business."

"You're the one who brought it up."

"Maybe I shouldn't have."

"Probably not. I don't care either way."

My hands fist at my sides. *This douche bag. This fucking... beast.* A run-of-the-mill jerk is just rude to you from the start. It takes a truly special kind of asshole to show you what could be possible—and then rip it all away just when you were starting to long for it.

He doesn't so much as pause as he heads for the door.

"Good! Go! Good fucking riddance!" I snap after him as he opens the door. "This is the last time we ever do this."

"We'll see about that, princess."

Then he's through the door, closing it and locking it behind him.

And leaving me alone with nothing but the angriest tears that have ever been cried.

"Mama," I murmur sadly to the empty stairwell, "what do I do?"

"Oh, my baby, my poor, poor baby..." she says in my head.

God, I'm weak. So stupid and weak. Talking to my imaginary mama—yep, hello, rock bottom. Nice to see you again.

"I'm sorry," I tell her. "I know this is pathetic. Crazy. I'm his prisoner, for God's sake."

"It's okay, my baby girl," she says in that lyrical voice of hers, smooth as guava butter. "There, there."

"You're not even real."

"Now, don't take this out on me," she scolds.

"I'm like a bipolar teenager. Second-guessing myself every two seconds. I thought I was beyond that. I thought I'd learned my lesson. That love isn't worth it."

Imaginary Mama sighs. "Don't you let me hear you say that again. Whatever mistakes your Papa made, those were his alone. And I made my fair share, too. Don't go learning things you have no business learning."

"If he had just—"

"We all do things we aren't proud of," she interrupts.

And then, suddenly, her voice changes.

It becomes my own—only shrill and hateful and accusing: *"Don't we, Melissa?"*

And just as suddenly, I'm shoved into a memory, blindsided with it like a hit I never saw coming.

I'm back, back there: the cool horror in my hands, the dank, choking stink of garbage, the grimy window and its sluggish light blaring in my eyes. The heat that sits on my sweaty body like a second layer of clothes. And the sobbing, pitched and wild, like a broken animal pleading for death in its own broken language…

No.

I throw myself upright, tottering and grabbing the railing. No. Not here. Not now.

I won't go back there. I can't.

"Kayla…" I whisper, desperate for a friend.

"Not you again," Imaginary Kayla says. "Get a hold of yourself, girl."

I try straightening my shoulders and standing up taller.

"There," she says approvingly. "That's better. This situation is fucked up, I'll give you that. But hey, what have our lives been the last ten years if not fucked up, am I right?"

"Yeah," I admit. "Just—"

"*Keep your head down and keep looking*—that was our motto, remember? Because if we never stop hoping and we never stop looking…"

"Then we won't miss the chance to escape when it comes," I finish for her.

"That's my girl," she croons. "Now, move your ass. Whatever Bastien Nikolaev is and whatever you do or do not feel for him, there's no point in sitting here obsessing over it."

I sigh. She's right. As I move to head down the stairs, the ceiling light overhead glints off something on the ground. I stare at it for a minute, sure I can't be seeing what I'm seeing.

It's key-colored, key-sized, and it's… holy shit, it is.

A brass key.

I shoot a suspicious, sidelong glance at the door. No way can this be happening. Bastien Nikolaev is at the top of his game. He outthinks me at every turn. Doesn't even trust me with fucking cutlery unless it's used under his supervision.

No goddamn way did he just so "happen" to "accidentally" drop the key to the basement door.

I pick it up slowly, still waiting for the door to fly open and show an ironically victorious or coldly angry Bastien.

I pause. Listen.

…

Nothing.

I take one step towards the door, then another. Jesus, am I really trying this?

Then again, what do I have to lose at this point? Oh, yeah—shower privileges. How horrifying. I would almost laugh right now if I wasn't so goddamn scared.

Right in front of the door now, I wait. I don't know what for, because nothing happens and nothing changes. Nothing but the increasing certainty that I have to try this.

Keep your head down and keep looking…

Only I think I've found it.

And now that I have, it's time. Time to try. Time to run.

Breath held, heart pounding, fingers shaking, I slip the key into the hole. It fits perfectly. I turn it and hear the click of freedom.

I push it open and then stand there for one wild moment looking at the dark rectangle where the door once was.

It can't be—can it?

I take one step out, just to be certain. All I have to do is dash to the front door and out into the world. Surely that's all it would take, right?

But the thump of one little thought resonates in my head over and over again.

It's a trap.

It's a trap.

It's a trap.

In the end, it's fear that wins. I close the door carefully. Then I put the key back in the keyhole, locking myself back in.

I clench it tight in my hand as I head back down the stairs, breathing hard like it's a bomb I'm holding. In a way, it is.

There's a voice in my head yelling: *Go now—run—escape! This is it! This is your chance!* But I can't risk it. Not until I'm certain he's out of the house and I'll have time to make it far, far away from here.

Besides, right now, I'm too tired to think properly. To decide just yet.

You only get one chance at escape. Screw it up and you won't get another.

I need to wait this out. I have to be sure that Bastien isn't in the house nor anywhere near it.

I settle on the bed with the ghost of a smile. The time will come soon enough. And then, finally, I'll be free.

A small, scared voice inside me whispers: *What happens after that?*

I force my smile to broaden and tell that little voice…

I haven't got that far yet. But something tells me that, whatever freedom's like, it's going to be amazing.

12

BASTIEN

I pull into my driveway and let out a weary sigh. It's only seven in the morning and yet I feel like this day will never end.

In the passenger seat next to me is a duffel bag filled with my bloodstained clothes. Not my blood—Cuban blood.

They never saw us coming. Or rather, they did, but only because we let them. That was the brilliance of the trap we sprung at the abandoned sheet metal factory where some of José's top lieutenants were holed up with guns, drugs, and girls.

Lukyan led a team in through the front doors. They acted stealthily enough for the Cubans to believe the threat was real, but it was all a ruse.

Because while chaos raged at the front, my own team went in through the windows of the upper stories. Silent enough that not even the rats noticed us creeping amongst the rafters.

When the Cubans came out spraying gunfire, Lukyan and his men ducked for cover.

And my men unleashed hell.

We rained bullets down for forty-five minutes, until nothing Cuban had a pulse any longer. Blood mixed with the dust on the factory floor and its stench filled the air.

Nothing ever smells sweeter.

I sigh again and step out of the car. I'm halfway to my front door when I hear the last voice I want to hear right now.

"Howdy, neighbor!"

Grimacing, I turn in place to see Randy on his commercial-ready lawn next door. He's on all fours pulling weeds, with a big, goofy sunhat like he's going on safari. Next to him, his dog is rolling on its back in the grass.

"Long day?" he jokes when he sees the expression on my face.

A small smirk touches my face as I consider how Randy would react if he had the foggiest idea of just what I got up to on my "long day."

"You could say that."

"Hate to be the bearer of bad news," he says cheerfully, "but it's about to get longer."

My eyes narrow into wary slits. What kind of bad news could this pink fuck have to deliver?

"What kind of bad news?"

"Well, I figured you got a new dog or something. Did ya?"

"No. Why?"

"Just heard banging and crashing earlier." He shrugs. "Thought it might be a new pup settling in. They can get rambunctious when they're youngins."

"No," I say, mind already racing and adrenaline firing up once again. It could be many things—Melissa escaping, the Cubans paying me a visit. Fuck. "Must be the contractors I hired. Renovations. Time to fix up the old basement. Excuse me."

I walk away. He says something behind me, but I ignore it. I have no fucking time for that shit. Not now.

Inside, I set the duffel bag down silently in the foyer and get out my gun. Creeping on quiet feet, I move from room to room with my weapon at the ready, finger on the trigger. Just how I was trained.

But nothing is out of place.

Living room, kitchen, bathroom, den—all empty. I go upstairs and check the other floors. Nothing there, either.

Only one place left to investigate.

I glide over to the basement, listening carefully, mind racing. Did she run? Is she dead?

I'm not sure which option is worse.

I pause by the door, turning my head so that my ear is near it, and listen. Nothing.

Then, with one hand, I open it and peer in. It's dark in the stairwell. Further down is just as dark.

I hear something. Just loud enough that it's audible, but quiet enough for me to have no fucking clue what it is.

I float down the stairs and turn the corner. One little light reflects off a shard of broken mirror lying on the bathroom floor. I see tufts of pillow stuffing strewn everywhere. Even the lid of the toilet hangs askew.

There wasn't much in here to destroy, but whoever did this was thorough about breaking what they could.

My first thought is Cubans. But my second thought, following right on its heels, says no.

It's her.

Deep in the gloom, I can just make her out: a huddling, whimpering ball. I holster my gun and straighten up. *What the fuck happened?*

I snap on the light, and do a three-sixty of the room. But sure enough, there's no one here. No one else could have done this.

I stride over. Melissa is a huddle of akimbo limbs, eyes squeezed shut. Her hair is a mess, her t-shirt rumpled. Her lithe arms are wrapped around her in a rigid semi-hug, holding herself like she's all she got left.

There's nothing visibly wrong with her. No blood, no bruising. I can see the soft motion of her breath.

But, *God...* She looks almost unrecognizable. Broken. Vulnerable.

Fuck that. I don't want to believe it. This stubborn mule actually breaking? No way. It must be that she just wants attention and so she threw a temper tantrum to get it.

The past few days after our encounter on the staircase, I've been cold with her. No reason to change that now.

And yet...

I find myself sitting beside her. When I put my hand on her shoulder, she flinches. Her head jerks to face me, eyes fluttering open blearily.

That's when I realize she's been asleep this whole time.

Her green eyes are bright with tears as they look at me miserably.

"What happened?" I ask.

Her lips tremble soundlessly around the syllables. She can't get the words out. Whatever it is, it's affecting her badly.

So I just react. I pull her into my lap and embrace her. Giving her something strong and unyielding she can cling to. I stroke her hair away from her face again and again.

"It's going to be alright," I murmur. "It's going to be okay."

Her sobbing gradually calms into whimpering. Her heartbeat stops stampeding.

And then, finally, silence.

She partially extricates herself from my lap, trying to look brave. "I'm fine."

She eyes me, trying to see if I'm buying it.

Nope. The ghost of pain on her face says she's not fine at all.

"What was all that about?" I rasp.

She pulls herself the rest of the way off of me with a shrug. "Something terrible happened to me once."

A long silence indicates that's all she's going to say about it. Well, that's a fucking rarity. Usually, this girl has everything to say about everything.

"And?" I press.

She frowns, studiously avoiding my eyes. "And I have night terrors about it sometimes, okay? Don't bother pretending to care."

"Who says I do? Who says I don't?"

"I'm your prisoner," she declares. "Nothing more."

"Stop it," I snap.

"Stop what?" she snaps right back.

I gesture at her. "This. Whatever it is."

"*Whatever it is,*" she mocks. "Let's stop whatever *this* is. Whatever we are, whatever we've been doing. What you've been doing to me."

"You're the one who said I've only been pretending to care," I say evenly.

"Yeah, and…?"

The strap of her sparkling bra dangles off one shoulder. The bare skin that I know is as soft as it looks is beckoning to me.

"And I think you want me to care," I say quietly.

The silence is like a knife blade the second it's serrated the skin. Before the blood comes.

And then she rounds on me, eyes blazing. "And why the hell would I want that, huh? I've been mistreated by mafia jerks my whole life. You're just another one!"

I catch her by the shoulder. "No. I am not."

She rips herself free, tears running down her upper cheeks now. I have to clench my fists to stop my hands from moving them to wipe them away.

"Yes, you are," she hisses. "You're no different. The whole lot of you. Fancying yourselves all righteous and moral, and doing the same shit anyway. Killing, hurting, taking what you want over and over again…" She trails off with a little shudder.

"You're wrong," I say gently. "I've never hurt a woman. Never."

"Bullshit."

"Look me in the eye and tell me I'm a liar."

"Or what, tough guy?" she demands. "You'll hit me?" Her nasty grin twists, eyes alight with devilish fire—she almost looks like she wants me to.

"Never," I say. "I'll never be like them."

"You're all the same," she says again. "Thinking you're in the right and doing all the wrong things."

I don't turn to face her. I heard the ironic certainty in her voice; no need to see it in her face.

"What about saving your life?" I ask. "Was that a 'wrong thing'?"

She doesn't answer.

"Or perhaps it's keeping you here that's wrong, hm? Perhaps I should've left you to one of my lieutenants to deal with."

She mutters something I can't hear.

I stalk around her. "It's a mistake that can easily be rectified, believe me."

"Do it, then!" she cries out angrily. "You want to get rid of me? Then get rid of me!"

She wraps her arms around herself and, crying harder now, face oddly still and prideful, sits herself back down on the mattress floor.

Looking down at her, I find all the angry responses I have fall away. She looks so… like she needs…

Don't go there, Bastien.

"You're just keeping me here because you're bored and want a distraction anyway," she continues.

"If I was bored and wanted a distraction," I growl, "you wouldn't be the one I choose."

"I don't know about that."

"You know nothing."

She laughs bitterly. "Of course I don't. I'm just a stupid little slave. No good for anything but following orders. It's all I've ever been."

I grit my teeth. "I don't expect you to understand the life I lead or the decisions I make."

Melissa rolls her eyes. "Of course you don't."

"People know what they are born into. What they are taught."

"And you're taught to kill, that crime is okay, is that it? You never had a choice but to do what you do? So sad. Also, so full of shit."

"You can put it like that," I say. "But the world isn't as black and white as they teach little kids. Bad men can do good things. Good men do bad things."

Melissa snorts. "Said every criminal ever."

I shrug. "I can't speak for them. But I can speak for myself. And I know I wouldn't be doing this if we were just out to hurt people. We help people, too."

She doesn't say anything for a while. Neither do I.

Whatever point I thought there was in talking through things with her, it hasn't served its purpose. If anything, it only riled her up more.

It's time to go.

I head for the stairs. The exhaustion sits heavily on my shoulders. I thought I was tired after the factory raid, but this is a whole new level of weariness.

"Why do you care about convincing me?" she calls out suddenly when I'm at the foot of the stairs.

"I don't know." I pause again. "Just... fuck, just come upstairs."

She eyes me warily. "And if I say no?"

"Then you'll be going without dinner. Your choice."

She glares at me, sits there without a word. I shrug and start heading up the stairs.

"Wait!" she says. "I'll come."

At the top of the stairs, I hold the door open. She comes slinking around the corner and up the steps. She keeps her eyes on me the whole time, a mouse watching a house cat and wondering when it's going to pounce.

But I don't. I stand perfectly still as she passes from the basement into the living room.

"Don't try anything," I say. "This is your only warning."

She rolls her eyes. "Scared I'll get one up on you?"

I shrug, heading for the kitchen. "Never underestimate your opponent."

Melissa snorts. "Oh, so that's what I am to you?"

I don't answer—mostly because I don't know how. What is Melissa to me?

That is one road I don't want to even begin to go down.

13

MELISSA

Do I dare?

I pause amidst cutting the carrots as the thought rolls through my head. The black plastic handle of the knife in my hand is slick with nervous sweat.

But almost as soon as I think the thought, I roll my eyes at myself.

Do I dare? Dare what—take on a man twice my size and strength with some takeout utensils?

Not unless I have a death wish.

I bury the daydream. But when I turn to face Bastien where he's leaning against the kitchen wall, observing me, I can see that he already knows what I was thinking.

"Good choice," he says.

I force my face into a confused, innocent expression. "Huh?"

He gestures to the knife in my hand. "If you had tried anything, I'd intercept you before you even had a chance to raise it."

"You really think I'm that slow?"

He smirks in that way I'm really starting to like: confident and brash. Like a big fuck-you to the world. "Try it."

His flashing dark eyes add: *I dare you.*

So I do.

I raise my arm, take one step forward, and—

BOOM—in the next second, his hand has closed around my wrist and twisted just enough that the knife falls from my grasp. His other arm hooks around my back, pressing me to him.

The second after that, our lips collide. His chest is taut against mine, his kiss soft yet firm. He kisses me like I'm his already. A demand. A promise.

He tastes like the Merlot he's been drinking, the same one he poured me a glass of that I've barely touched. Weirdly enough, kissing makes me feel drunker than the wine did.

Or maybe I'm just drunk on him. His dark musk. His dark, swirling, smoky—

Wait.

That's not a smoky smell. That's *smoke.*

"Damn it!" I exclaim. We spin apart to see the stir fry oil on fire in the pan on the burner.

I rush over to grab it and shove the flaming pan under the faucet, throwing the water on. As the water extinguishes the fire and hisses like an alley cat, I can't help but start laughing.

"I blame you, you know," I say. "For distracting me."

Behind me, I can hear Bastien chuckling as he goes back to cutting up the chicken. "Not my fault you're so easily distracted."

"And it's not my fault you're so…" I trail off, not sure how I want to finish that sentence. Or if I even know how to.

"Funny? Charming? Devilishly handsome?"

"Arrogant, is what I was gonna say."

"The fact that that distracts you says more about you than it does about me."

I roll my eyes, but I'm laughing again. Returning to the cutting board, I resume slicing the carrots. "Bet you never dreamed you'd be making dinner with your prisoner."

Bastien snorts. "I never dreamed I'd be making dinner with any woman."

"Oh yeah? What makes me so special?"

It was mostly a joke, but when I glance over, I see a serious frown on his face.

"Well?"

He just shrugs, then keeps on cutting the chicken.

"That's it?" I press. "Come on. Give me a little bit more, Mr. Strong and Silent."

"I was attracted to you when I first saw you in that club," he admits.

I laugh. "That's what the skimpy outfits are for."

"It wasn't that." *Chop-chop-chop.* His knife on the board is quick and efficient.

"Then what was it?"

Chop-chop-chop. Another shrug.

"Bastien," I grumble.

He sighs and sets the knife down. "You had spirit."

"*Spirit?*" I repeat dubiously.

"That's what I said." He's not looking at me, though I'm sure looking at him. "Feistiness. Bravery."

A fluttery feeling erupts in my chest. "Aw, are you going soft on me, Bastien Nikolaev?"

He scowls. "Don't count on it."

"I was only joking," I say softly, starting to cut again.

This time, he turns and fixes me with a look that makes my ovaries burn. "Be careful what you joke about, princess."

We finish cutting up the vegetables and chicken in a strained sort of silence. I toss in the haphazard mix of spices Mama always hinted at and never outright confirmed and try to pretend like I'm fine with the quiet.

When Bastien leaves for the bathroom, I lean on the marble gray and white countertop to survey the room.

It's a nice kitchen. Huge, really. About the size of my old apartment, give or take. Which says more about the tininess of my apartment than the bigness of this place, but still.

As for the rest of the place, it's sparsely furnished. No pictures, no signs that it's anything other than a model home.

Unexpected tears spring to my eyes. I quickly blink them back. It takes me a few seconds to realize why.

It's the smell. The rich mix of the stir fry's vegetables and herb chicken reminds me of her, no matter how often I make it. My mama.

"Loafing on the job?" Bastien jokes as he strides back in. His look, though, is serious, intent. Like trying to figure out a puzzle.

It comes to me with a cold slap: Bastien was just gone a good five minutes, and I spent the whole freaking time *admiring his kitchen* instead of doing the obvious: trying to escape.

Worst of all? It didn't even cross my mind.

"The dinner is pretty much prepped. Just a few minutes more and it'll be all cooked, too," I point out, gesturing to the steaming pan. "And besides, I thought you could handle the cutlery."

Bastien's dark brows raise. "Aren't you supposed to be the prisoner?"

"Aren't you supposed to be keeping me under a tight lock and key?"

"Don't tempt me."

"Do your worst. As long as you leave my hands free so I can eat my stir-fry."

"And miss out on sitting in my mostly untouched dining room? It can wait." Bastien hooks his arm through mine and he leads me to the dining room to gesture grandly some exquisitely carved mahogany wooden chairs and tabletop.

"Very impressive, sir."

"The bedroom is even better."

My cheeks bloom red immediately. I'm in the midst of figuring out what the hell to say to *that* when I hear a *BEEP-BEEP-BEEP* from the kitchen.

"That's the timer I set," I say, extricating myself hastily to go over and turn off the burner. "One fire for the day is enough, I think."

"Should've used the first one when you had the chance."

"Huh?" I ask, wrinkling my nose.

"If you'd let it go off, you might've escaped," Bastien points out.

"Don't tempt me," I say, throwing his own words back at him. "Anyway, if I do try to escape, it will be when you least expect it."

His eyebrow arches. "Is that so?"

"Big time. You'll never see it coming."

"I think you'd be surprised by what I see coming, princess." Bastien's smile drops away. His eyes are suddenly as hard and indifferent as coal.. "But I meant what I said. If I catch you escaping once, that's it for these favors."

I frown. "You say that like these 'favors' are all for me. Please—as if you would do favors for some prisoner you didn't give a damn about."

"Don't presume to know what I do and don't give a damn about, Melissa."

I shiver the way I always do when he says my name like that. Laced with threat.

Bastien goes to the table and sits down, powerful hands flat on its surface. "I'm ready when you are."

"Well, the meal isn't," I grumble, even though it is. "You'll just have to wait."

I turn and busy myself with poking the food around in the pan a little more, if only because I need to collect myself before I go sit with him.

I'm standing in this man's kitchen and joking around with him like we're some normal, domestic couple in some normal, domestic world. But nothing about this is normal. I'm a prisoner and he's my captor.

And there's a key tucked under my mattress that would end this all so easily.

So why haven't I used it? More to the point, why haven't I so much as *thought* about using it?

I shudder and spoon the finished food into the waiting bowls. I can't think about this right now. It's too big, too painful, too confusing.

The aroma hits my senses as I carry our food over to the table and sit.

"This is good," Bastien admits after a few bites. "Damn good."

"My mama was a good cook," I say quietly. "Good at anything she put her mind to, really. Most of my qualities that I'm proud of are from her."

"Like your voice."

"Yeah," I say with a soft laugh. "Nice of her to share that with me."

"You ever think of doing it professionally?"

"You mean when I'm free of the mob du jour?" I retort. "Yeah, actually. Thought it might be fun. If I ever get the chance."

"Hm."

I continue, "My friend Kayla and I always had this dream. It was more mine, really—she just wanted to be near me. We'd have this club called The Rainbow. It'd have an eclectic mix of genres and music. Everyone would be welcome, young and old, every race, every gender. Maybe not kids, obviously, but pretty much everyone else otherwise. We'd have emo nights, swing dancing nights, rap nights, rave nights. People would just come and enjoy themselves. Be themselves…" I trail off, my gaze falling to my almost untouched plate. "It's just a silly pipe dream, though."

I've picked up my fork and stabbed a forkful of carrots, beans, and chicken, when Bastien says, "No."

I don't put the bite in my mouth. "You don't have to humor me."

"I'm not."

"Then why…" I trail off as his hand finds mine, squeezes it.

"I'd go."

I bite my lip. I want to say something real, something genuine myself, like *You mean it? What else are you thinking?*

But I stamp it back. "Do you even go out?" I tease instead.

His smile disappears. "Not if I can help it."

"Why not? Afraid that you'll have too much fun?"

"Something like that."

I sigh, picking back up my fork. "What *do* you do for fun, then? Behead traitors?"

"Nah, I prefer slowly burning them to death."

"You know," I say, "that joke's almost not funny when you're actually a mafia killer."

Bastien shrugs. "I do what I have to."

"Yeah, yeah," I say. "But what about what you *want* to do?"

His dark brows knit together.

"What?" I ask. "Did I say a bad word?"

Bastien just sighs "There will be time enough for what I want when my empire is secured."

I make a dubious face. "You're telling me that, before this war with the Cubans and whatever other wars you Bratva guys were involved in, you knew how to have fun?"

"If you're asking did I party," Bastien says, "then the answer is no. My brother, Gavriil, on the other hand, lives for the clubs. Used to, at least."

"Not anymore?"

"Married and thrilled about it," he says with a grimace.

"Some people like that, you know."

"Not me," he says. "I find other things fun."

"Like what? You don't strike me as, like, an artist."

"You're wrong." He inclines his head. "Art, concerts. The shooting range."

I make a face at that last one. "I should've guessed. You like imagining the targets are your enemies?"

"You don't have to keep repeating yourself," Bastien scowls. "You don't like what I do. I get it. Lucky for us both, it's not up to you."

"Lucky for me?" I roll my eyes. "In what world am I lucky?"

Bastien leans over the table so we're close. "You know José Correa better than me, so you tell me: what do you think a city run by him would be like? Nice and wholesome? Safe for all the little boys and girls?"

His cutting dark eyes know the answer already. I look away.

"No," I say quietly.

"Speaking of which," Bastien says, voice cold now. "Before, you were telling me about how much you knew about the Cubans, about how useful you could be. But so far, all I've heard about is how terrible it is that I'm a man of the Bratva. How about you start delivering what was promised?"

My hand tightens on my fork as I glare at him. "You haven't asked."

"I'm asking now."

I fiddle with my fork, resisting the urge to shovel half of my stir-fry into my mouth at once. Stress eating is not a good look.

"There's not much more to know than what you've probably already heard. José is a control freak. A details junkie. Doesn't try any of the drugs, throws out his boys who do. He's merciless. He doesn't trust anyone."

"That could describe almost anyone," Bastien says. "Tell me more. Girls? Friends? Confidantes?"

"They all died in 'accidents,'" I recount quietly. "Apparently, other people were just getting in the way. There may be truth to it, since after they died, José only got stronger. Or it could just be the fear. Everyone's terrified of him."

He nods. "So no girls."

"None that José keeps around very long. He sees them as a liability." I eye him, trying to place the look on his face. Then I see it. "You think he's smart for that, don't you?"

"Many a greater man has come to his ruin thanks to distractions."

I try to keep my voice light, but I can't keep the edge out of it. "That's all 'women' are to you? A distraction?"

Bastien picks up his fork again and stabs through several pieces of chicken at once. "Not this again."

"Yes, *this again*." I can feel it, building in my belly like a storm I can't stop. The anger. The frustration. Why do I even care and why can't I stop it? "You really can't talk about personal things, ever?"

"Not when they all seem to circle back to you and me," he says.

"And what's wrong with that?"

He just keeps chewing and doesn't answer..

"Forget it," I snap. "I know where I stand. You don't need to remind me."

Prisoner.

At his mercy.

Helpless.

And yet, if I don't need reminding, then why the hell do I keep bringing it up?

We sit there, eating in silence. Bastien's chewing is merciless, practical. Like he's trying to annihilate even his food.

The quiet lasts until Bastien's phone goes off. He glances at it and rises.

"I have to get this." He eyes me thoughtfully. "It might take a while."

"I can get started on dessert?" I offer.

"No." He takes something out of his pocket. His phone is still ringing, but he switches it to silent. Then he shows me what's in his hand.

Cuffs.

My stomach plummets.

"You going to fight me on this?" he asks.

"No," I whisper.

He nods. "Good."

Stooping over, he fastens one cuff around the leg of the insanely heavy table—no way will I be able to lift it to slide it off—and locks the other around my ankle.

Then he straightens and gazes down at me. There's a half-second when I think he's about to say something or do something...

But then he turns away and heads to the hallway.

"So glad you trust me!" I call after him.

He says nothing as he disappears from view.

I sigh, looking around the room. It's chrome everywhere. A chrome dishwasher and a chrome fridge and a chrome oven and a bunch of matching chrome appliances: toaster, blender, microwave, coffee maker. There's even a chrome phone on the counter to my left.

I freeze, my gaze snapping that way.

A chrome phone on the counter to my left.

It's there. Right freaking *there* and if I just stretch my free arm a bit as far as I can, I can maybe grab it.

"If I catch you escaping once, that's it for these favors," Bastien's gruff voice echoes in my head.

But that isn't what's holding me back, I realize with a scowl. That isn't what's making me hover my fingers above the phone like I'm an idiot who doesn't know how to use it.

It's the look of disappointment that would be on his face when he found out.

"You're his prisoner, Melissa," I hiss to myself. "That's all you are to him. That's all you'll ever be to him."

And still, I hesitate. Bastien isn't stupid. Him dropping the key was just a fluke. A mistake. What are the chances he'd be careless enough to make two?

Which means, if this isn't another mistake, then it's something else.

A test.

I sigh. The truth is, there's only one call I want to make—need to make—and no risk is going to stop me.

I pick up the phone.

14

BASTIEN

In the study, I start to pace, eyeing the phone on my desk.

Soon, but not yet. I have a different call to make first.

"Hey," Dmitry says, picking up the phone.

"Hey. You called?"

"You busy?"

"In the middle of something, but it can wait."

"Mother wanted me to call," Dmitry admits. "Says you've been ducking her."

"She needs to let me do my job."

"You know her. She's just worried," he says. "You're lucky she's not in the same city as you."

"Don't give her any ideas," I snap. "She's been trying to invite herself down here since the start."

"That does sound like something she'd do."

"If you know anything about the situation," I say gruffly, "then you know that this is the last place she should be."

"Agreed," Dmitry says. "We don't want a repeat of our last family dinner."

"Gavriil still hasn't lived that one down."

"Although business in Boston is booming," Dmitry says, a note of respect in his voice. "I have to say, he impressed me with how he turned it around at the end there. With your help, of course."

"I'm assuming you're calling to talk about here, not there?"

Normally, I'd engage in some idle chit-chat, but now really isn't the time. My gaze strays to the office telephone on my mahogany wood desk. I can feel my chest clench with anticipation.

"Awfully touchy today, are we?"

"You only ever lead off with small talk when you're about to follow it up with some unsolicited advice."

"That's the only kind I can give to you, brother," he chuckles. "I can't remember you ever asking for advice, ever."

"I seek it when it is needed," I say simply. "Too many rely on others to do their thinking for them. A dangerous habit to pick up."

"You sound like Father. But fine, fine, we'll cut the small talk. Onto business: I hear you have a prisoner."

I roll my eyes. "For fuck's sake, not you, too."

Dmitry laughs. "You know Gavriil can't keep a secret for shit."

"It's not a secret."

"Oh?"

"No," I say, my teeth on edge. "It's an inconvenience, that's all. One I won't let get in the way of what I have to do. What I have to focus on."

"I never doubted it for a second, brother," Dmitry says. "It's just…"

"Then what is this call about?"

"Just to make sure you don't stay focused on empire-building to the exclusion of all else."

"You and Gavriil have your own ways of getting things done," I tell him. "Mine is focusing on what I want until I get it. Anything else is just a distraction."

"What does that make the girl?"

"What does it matter? She's a prisoner."

He sighs and is quiet for a few moments. "Nina wasn't your fault, Bastien."

My teeth grit harder. "You know I don't talk about her."

"As you wish," Dmitry says simply. "But you know Father's stance on it."

"As lovely as this has been, brother, I have to go," I say. "There's no time for distractions now. You can tell that to Mother if she asks why she can't visit."

"Alright," Dmitry says. "Stay safe, Bastien. And if you need help, or advice, or anything, really…"

"I'll let you know," I say.

We hang up. Irritation brews in my stomach, but I set it aside. It's time for what comes next.

Seeing Melissa's reaction when I left the kitchen gave me an idea: if I left her in the same room as the phone, alone, would she use it?

I check my watch. She's had just enough time to hem and haw. If she's going to do it, it's going to be now.

I pick up the landline and listen.

Will she or won't she? Can I trust her or can I not?

It would be all too easy for her to call the Cubans and tell them where she is. I didn't have her blindfolded when I took her here. She might even know the exact address.

But even if she doesn't call them up, that doesn't mean that keeping her here is anything other than a bad idea. The way she gets to me...

My hands grip the phone hard. And then I hear it.

The click. The breathing.

She's picked up the phone, is on the line, thinking it over right now. She must've been thinking it over for a good while if she's waited until now to finally make her move.

The dial tone sounds out into the tense silence. *Brrr. Brrr.*

Followed by the click of an answer.

"Hey, who is this?" an unfamiliar female voice asks.

"Kayla?" Melissa breathes.

"Jesus—Mel? Is that you?" The voice—Kayla's—sounds shocked, overjoyed.

"Yeah, it's me, Kay." Melissa laughs raggedly. "I don't have a lot of time, but yeah, it's me. God, I sat here for minutes trying to work up the courage, holding the phone like an idiot... but I'm babbling. Yeah, it's me."

"So you *are* alive!" Kayla exclaims. "God, I'm so relieved. I thought—I was worried they... It doesn't matter now. Where are you? What's happening? Let me come get you!"

Melissa pauses. I clench the phone tight in my hand, waiting for her answer.

Yes, for the love of God, please come get me.

Instead...

"How are you?" she finally asks.

"Is he listening?" Kayla demands. "Is that fucking Russian asshole forcing you to do this, to send us a message?"

"No, nothing like that," Melissa says, almost laughing. "Just, I wanted to know: are you okay? The club..."

"Is reduced to what it should've been years ago," Kayla finishes firmly. "A smoking pile of rubble. But don't worry, they found a new seedy club for me to work at. Hired a bunch of bimbos to stand in for you and Antonia, but the men hate them."

I chuckle. "I'll bet."

"I miss you," Kayla whines. "The apartment feels so empty without you singing and cooking."

"We'll get to see each other again, Kay. I promise."

"You sure?" Kayla says.

"A thousand percent," Melissa says. "Maybe it's stupid, but it's a feeling I can't shake. Or, shit, maybe it's just desperation and hope speaking, who knows. I just can't imagine never seeing you again."

"Me neither," Kayla says. "I hate this. It really feels eerie without you waking me up, yelling at me that I'm going to be late for work if I don't move my ass." She chuckles, though it quickly tapers off. "But where are you? José is still really pissed about what happened. If you told me where you were, they could have guys down there fast and unexpected. The Russians would never see it coming—"

"Don't," Melissa says, sounding tired now. "Just... don't."

Kayla sighs. "I just want you back home safe and sound, girl. Where you belong."

"We didn't belong there," Melissa replies. "Not with them."

"No," Kayla says softly. "Maybe not. But at least we had each other."

"Yeah. That's something."

Background scuffle comes from Kayla's end of the phone.

"Where are you, anyway?" Melissa asks.

"I'm at that new club I was talking about, El Paradiso—real original, right?" Kayla says with a snort. "They serve this coconut shrimp that's actually pretty good, but you won't believe what some of the men get up to with the sticks they come with. And that guava lotion? José's replaced it with something even worse—fake banana scented shit. I swear, some nights I feel like I'm actually going to vomit. And the regulars here are worse, complete handsy pervs. We've doubled our security to deal with them. Guess they got kicked out of El Palacio when it was full and crawled their way here. Anyway, you caught me at a good time. I'm on my break, but I only have five more minutes or so. José is as much of a time-keeping douche bag as ever. He has us punch in and out like we're goddamn grocery store clerks. Hell, he's had two of the girls smacked up several times for being late already. Oh, wait—No! No—"

More noise. Quieter voices that I can't hear from the background.

"Melissa, so glad to hear from you," a gravelly Spanish-accented voice drawls. "But from what Kayla's telling me… it sounds like you've forgotten all we did for you already."

A sharp exhale of breath—Melissa's.

Then the call ends abruptly.

I stand there for a few seconds to process, then hang up my handset slowly.

That was… enlightening? Something like it, at least. Melissa says she feels safer here than she did with the Cubans. Unless she knew I was listening and modified her responses accordingly? If that's the case, why bother calling at all, then?

I rise with a scowl. Enough pointless thinking. Time to get back to the kitchen. See what happens. See what she's capable of.

If Melissa pretends she didn't use the phone, she can't be trusted. If she admits it—well, she still can't be.

I stride out of the study. Looks like it's no trust either way.

And yet…

As I head into the kitchen, I shake the thought aside. Better not think about it.

"Missed me?" Melissa quips as I undo the handcuffs and our arms brush.

"No," I say as I sit down at the table across from her.

"Liar."

"Let's just eat," I say.

We just eat. I do, at least. The whole time, Melissa keeps glancing up at me, biting her lip, hardly touching her food at all.

"Good call?" she asks finally.

"Good enough," I say. "Good wait?"

"Good enough." She glances away, at her feet, the floor, the food on her plate.

"You look nervous," I observe neutrally, putting down my fork.

"I *am* nervous." The look that crosses her face is almost relieved at being called out.

"Why?"

"Because I called my friend," she blurts out.

Our gazes catch. Hers hasn't decided what it is, yet. Mine neither.

"Why?" I ask evenly.

"Because I missed her, I think," Melissa says, voice defiant, though her eyes stay locked on her plate. "Because she was the only one who cared about me back home. Because I just… wanted to hear a friendly voice."

I incline my head. "Understandable. What did you tell her?"

"Nothing, really. I just wanted to make sure that she was okay. And to let her know that I was okay, too."

I say nothing. I'm watching for cracks in her armor, tells in her demeanor. I've spent a lifetime studying people and learning how to read them.

In her, though, I'm seeing nothing but the truth.

One of her green eyes is half-squinted in thought as she studies me back. "You don't look surprised."

I shrug. "I'm not."

"Why?"

"I listened to the call in the other room."

"What?" she exclaims. "You lied!"

"And you disobeyed my orders."

Her gaze snaps up and faces off against mine, but then it drops without another word of protest.

"That's it?" I ask. "Unlike you to not have something quippy to say."

She glares at me. "Am I going to lose shower and dinner privileges now?"

"Perhaps. I haven't decided. But first, there's something I want to know." I lean forward and prop my elbows on the table. "Why didn't you tell him?"

"Tell him what?"

"Where you were, where to find you. He could've rescued you."

"Rescued me." She laughs, finally eyeing me derisively. "You mean free me so I can be his slave instead? Gee, how tempting."

"Why not get your friend to call the police for you, then?" I press. "Then you could've been truly free."

This laugh is sadder, as is the shake of her head that sends her sandy ponytail swinging. "Not in this city, no. Like I told you, José is a control freak. He'd never just let me go. And you and your men…" She looks up at me with a hard emerald gaze. "Something tells me that you wouldn't take my escape well. No, people like me and Kayla, we don't pull the strings. Best thing to do is to go along with those who do, as long as we can. Unless the perfect chance presents itself."

"Pretty speech," I murmur. "Too bad I don't believe a word of it."

Her gaze slips to me with sudden anger. "Why?"

"Because I don't think *you* believe a word of it."

She chews on that for a minute. Picks at her bottom lip with one long nail. "Maybe I don't know myself, okay?" she whispers. "Maybe I'm just scared. Or stupid. Or maybe I know all too well what the Cubans are capable of."

"Tell me."

"No," she snaps, on her feet now. "I've had enough of this. I failed your little test, okay? Now, take what you want from me, whatever it is. Take away my shower privileges, send me back to the basement—just leave me the hell alone and stop messing with my head."

I rise to glower down on her. Part of me wants to take her by the arm, bend her over my knee, and...

No. I tuck my hands in my pockets before they make a mistake.

"I need to know what I'm dealing with," I tell her quietly.

"What *you're* dealing with?" she hisses. "Here's a word for you: monsters. Evil fucks who dragged me and Mama into their filthy club basement and then—"

Before she can finish her story, there's a noise.

Glass shattering.

"How" and "where" don't matter—the only thing that matters is moving. I grab Melissa and hustle her to the downstairs bathroom.

I shove her in, growl, "Don't move," and slam the door shut before she can even process what's happening. Then I rip my gun out of my holster and race back out.

Upstairs reveals nothing. All I can see out the window is a flock of plastic flamingos my neighbor has planted in his front yard. The other way shows only the rolling hill that borders the neighborhood. No cars, no pedestrians.

I turn and descend the stairs. I'm halfway down the hallway when I hear it—pounding on the door.

Who's here, and what the fuck do they want?

Doesn't matter. Whoever it is, it's his funeral.

I lift my gun and point it at the front door. I'll empty the clip if that's what it takes. Messy, but it's not like I'd be staying here after. Not after this major fucking security breach.

I'm three steps away from the door. Two. One.

And then, before I can reach it, the doorknob turns.

I left it unlocked.

I'm so stunned by my idiotic rookie mistake—who the fuck leaves the door of a safehouse unlocked?—that I can only stand in place, slack-jawed, as the door swings inward.

Until there's no time to hide, no time to take cover.

There's only time to do one thing: raise my gun and kill whoever the hell is about to step foot in my house.

15

MELISSA

I lean against the porcelain sink and count my breaths the way I always do when I think a panic attack is coming on.

And yet, it never comes. My breathing isn't harried. My heart isn't even beating fast.

Why am I not more scared? I should be ducking for cover at the very least, trying to hide in the shower or something.

The answer is obvious: I trust Bastien.

He's murderous, dangerous, and... eminently capable. Whoever's shown up here is going to get a nasty surprise.

My momentary peace quivers as Bastien's footfalls slam on the floor above me, changing direction. I try to keep breathing and brace for the noise. For the shooting that somehow still hasn't started.

What will I do when it does? Am I really just going to leave Bastien to deal with the Cubans himself? He may be capable, but no amount of capability can help you if you're outnumbered ten to one.

That's the thing about José: he doesn't fight fair. If he sent men here, it wouldn't be just one or two—it would be as many killers as he could cram into a speeding SUV. A whole caravan's worth. An army of vicious bastards.

Above, I can hear shouting. I pause, making out the words.

Is that...

It is.

Randy, Bastien's neighbor.

It sounds like he's yelling. "Jesus, Bastien! Please! Oh, God, please! Don't shoot!"

Oh, shit. I rush out of the bathroom, up the stairs and to the front door, skidding to a stop at what I see.

Bastien has his muscled forearm across Randy's beefy chest and his gun dug in deep into his flank. There's a savagery in his dark eyes that's almost animal.

"What the hell are you doing here?" Bastien roars at Randy.

"I'm sorry...!" Randy whimpers.

"Fuck your sorry!" Bastien yells again. "Who sent you?"

Randy's face is purpling as he wheezes, "I... can't breathe..."

Bastien lets up pressure slightly, although his yell is as enraged as ever. "Who the fuck sent you?"

"I just wanted to get my golf ball, okay?" Randy gasps, his double chin shaking with the effort of coughing. "I'm sorry! I shouldn't have opened the door! I don't know what I was thinking!"

"No shit you shouldn't have," Bastien growls.

Golf ball...

I turn and race for the kitchen, and, sure enough, there it is. A golf ball sitting placidly on the tile under the kitchen table. We must've missed it. Assumed the worst when we heard the impact through the window.

I pick it up and hurry back to the front door. If I don't do something now, this innocent moron is going to end up with enough holes in him to pass for Swiss cheese. I saw the look on Bastien's face. He isn't playing around, and he isn't capable of seeing the intruder—however innocuous—as anything other than a threat.

So it's intervene, or Randy dies.

I reach the foyer and rest my fingertips on Bastien's forearm. "Bastien, let him go."

Bastien grunts, face still twisted with rage.

"Please," I add quietly.

No reaction. God, there has to be something I can do or say to make him let go, move.

"It's from serving overseas," I explain to Randy in a fast, tense voice. "PTSD. Bastien hears a loud noise and he just... snaps. I'm so sorry. We're trying therapy and it's helping, but..."

My heart is beating so hard against my chest it feels like something foreign. Like even it knows this situation is beyond repair.

I give Bastien's arm another squeeze. It's all taut muscle. "Bastien, please."

One glance at his profile and it's obvious how much of a lost cause this is. His face is still twisted with that same unhearing rage.

I stand on tiptoe so my lips are at his ear. "Please, Bastien. For me."

It's stupid and ridiculous—Bastien's already made it painfully clear what we are and aren't. What we'll never be. *"For me?"* Might as well say "for Randy's cute sheepdog" for as much good as it'll do me.

And yet, a long time passes in those few seconds. Enough that I wonder if Bastien is actually considering my words.

His face softens from its inhuman, brutal expression. His grip loosens. And then, finally—*no damn way*—he lets go.

I don't realize how little I expected that until I'm practically gasping in relief, along with Randy, who's gasping in a more literal sense. I'm honestly shocked he hasn't pissed himself.

"Yes, we really are so, so sorry," I blab on, mostly so Randy won't say anything that could make this even worse. "Some of the things Bastien saw over there... God, I can't even tell you. It's remarkable he's even with us today. A real war hero. But the PTSD... I'm so, so sorry."

I shoot a warning glare at Bastien. "Yes. Randy, I..." He clears his throat and straightens his shoulders. "I owe you an apology. I overreacted."

Understatement of the century, but it could work... maybe?

I scan Randy's face nervously. He still looks so focused on the problem of breathing that he hasn't even begun to consider how he feels about this at all.

"It's... okay," Randy finally says with a forced laugh that might just be a cough. "I shouldn't have gone waltzing into your house, door open or no. People can be finicky about those kinds of things. My old Aunt Jemma, for instance, she wouldn't have even bothered to tackle me. Ninety-seven, more than half-deaf, but wary as a prairie cat. She woulda picked up that old Winchester rifle she kept by the door and boom!—no more Randy."

His laughing sounds more real, though partially hysterical. Not that I blame him. If I just got nearly murdered by my neighbor, I'd be pretty shook up about it, too.

"Do you need help getting home?" I ask him. "We really are so sorry."

"No, no." Randy straightens up and wipes his sweaty brow. "I'm the one who is sorry."

"Let us make it up to you," I continue with a desperate smile. "Would you be up for some coffee and cookies in a bit? Bastien has the best oatmeal raisin cookies, you'll see. Just give us ten minutes or so to get tidied up and put a pot of coffee on. Your wife is welcome, too, of course."

Seconds tick away. Hopefully, Randy's trying to decide whether to take me up on my offer, and not which believable lie he can tell us before hurrying back home to call the cops.

"Yeah, you know what?" Randy finally says, starting to smile. "We'll do that. And I'll bring my wife's favorite chocolate chai tea as well. You'll see—there's nothing like it. See you in ten."

As soon as he's gone and Bastien has closed the door after him, he rounds on me. "What the fuck was that?"

I stare at him for a good few seconds before it occurs to me that he's actually serious. The man is actually pissed at me.

"Oh, you mean me cleaning up your mess?" I hiss. "Really, a simple 'thank you' would suffice. Mr. Paranoid over here thought a stray golf ball was a Cuban raid and nearly put a bullet hole in an innocent man!"

"I'm not paranoid."

"Call it what you like then."

I realize I'm still touching him at the same time he does. He looks down at my fingers resting against his elbow, grimaces, and shrugs me off.

Guess that answers it: back to the basement it is for the prisoner.

But then he sighs and his forehead eases. "For fuck's sake."

"You're just stressed," I say quietly. "It's understandable."

"You don't know what I am."

"I never said I did. But I do know it's not normal when someone reacts like that, mobster or no. So excuse me for giving you the benefit of the doubt."

"Excused," he drawls. He's wavering back and forth between caustic and kind, like he can't decide who to blame for this debacle. He looks at me and tilts his head to the side like he's trying to puzzle something out. "Why didn't you run?"

"Huh?"

"You could've taken that chance to escape, when I was busy with Randy."

"Should I have scooted around the crazed Russian Bratva boss with a gun in his hand and his finger on the trigger?"

"You could've gone out the back."

"Why? Are you wishing I did? Save you the trouble?"

Bastien exhales. "Why does everything between us have to end in a fight?"

"Maybe because half the time when I'm with you, I feel like I'm being interrogated," I suggest acidly.

Bastien doesn't say anything to that. Although his mouth moves in a way that could be a distant relative to a smile.

"What were you saying, before the golf ball," he says. "About what the Cubans—"

Ding-dong, chimes the doorbell. *Ding-dong, ding-dong.*

Our eyes meet. I guess we shouldn't be surprised that Randy and his wife were so eager that they came over in closer to five minutes than ten.

"Tell you later," I say. "I'll go clean up the floor."

Bastien nods and heads to the door. Seconds later, I hear it opening, followed by happy voices.

After quickly sweeping up the broken glass, I head to the door to see Randy, accompanied by a trim blonde woman with a beaming smile.

"First things first," she says with a chuckle. "Randy told me what happened, and I just about laughed my head off. You won't believe how many times I got after him about practicing in our backyard. And every time, it was the same ol' song and dance: *I'll be careful, honey, you've nothing to worry about, yadda, yadda, yadda*—Well, anyway, we're both really, truly sorry. Let us know how much the repairs cost and Randy will pay you back."

Bastien grunts his assent, while I say, "Don't worry about it. We're sorry for Bastien's overreaction, too."

Her china blue gaze lands on me. "You must be Melissa. It's a pleasure. I'm Amy."

"Nice to meet you, Amy," I say. "Despite the circumstances."

She laughs as she moves forward to shake my hand. Her grip is soft yet firm. "Well, if that's what got us to finally have a nice, neighborly coffee chat, then so be it!"

"We actually didn't have time to get out the cookies or even clear our dinner plates or anything," I tell them as we pass the kitchen. "So maybe setting ourselves up on the outdoor patio would be best? It's a really beautiful evening outside."

"Sounds lovely, dear," she agrees.

Bastien detours to the kitchen to get a tin of cookies and some mugs for the tea while the rest of us head outside to sit on the wicker patio furniture. When he emerges, he pours four cups for us.

"Bastien was just telling me that this was a family recipe," Randy says as he sits down beside his wife, mid-chew. "His mother's worried about him, so she sends cookies."

"New city," Bastien says brusquely. "You know how it is."

"You never mentioned what you do exactly," Randy says. "What brought you to Miami, anyway?"

"I'm part of the family business," Bastien says easily. "Although I'm currently still recovering from..." He shoots me a sidelong look. "My service."

Amy nods. "We completely understand. Serving our country, you should be proud. Goodness knows we appreciate the troops in our household."

Bastien just grimaces as he reaches for a cookie.

Randy's already chowed down two and a half of them. "Any chance of getting your mother's recipe?" he asks. "The woman's a genius. Can't remember the last time I had cookies this good."

"I'll ask," Bastien says. "But she can be fiercely protective sometimes."

"I'll bet," Amy says with a sympathetic smile. "Maybe she'll pass the secret down to you, Melissa."

Bastien stiffens. "They haven't... met quite yet."

Randy just laughs, patting him. "I know how it is. New relationships, you have to feel them out first. How long have you two been together, anyway?"

I glance at Bastien. Based on his less-than-enthusiasm to me taking initiative, I'm going to leave this one to him.

"A little over a month," Bastien answers.

"Well, you two seem like quite the pair, from what I heard about from Randy," Amy says kindly, sipping her tea. "All over each other. And just looking at the pair of you, anyone can see how crazy Bastien is about you. So protective. It's sweet."

I sip my tea, trying to hide my smile. Amy Finch, with her light pink paisley print dress and genuine, happy blue eyes, looks like someone who believed in Santa Claus until oh, about age thirty or so. What does she know about love or affection or the danger that hides in every damn shadow in this city?

Not a damn thing.

But that doesn't stop my heart from fluttering in the strangest way. I decide to ignore it.

"How did you two meet?" Randy asks.

"At the club," I say. Number one rule of lying: make up as little as possible.

"She was dancing with some friends," Bastien adds.

"He was there with a group of his friends, too," I add. "They didn't seem to be a fan of the music—or the club."

"Maybe if you girls hadn't been requesting back-to-back Enrique Iglesias," Bastien retorts.

I laugh. "Better than those PitBull songs you all insisted on badgering the poor DJ to play."

It's all playing out in my head, almost as if it were real: the music, the boys, Bastien, me. Lights. Drinks. Freedom.

"Anyways," I continue, "we made a bet on a coin flip. Heads, and my friends and I got our songs. Tails, and the boys got to choose. Only, at the last second—coin was in mid-air and everything!—Bastien added to it: tails and he got to take me out. I agreed, and..."

"I guess it was tails?" Amy interrupts excitedly.

"No, actually," Bastien replies. "It was heads. But I'm not the kind of man who gives up so easily."

"And the rest was history," I finish.

With the two of us recounting the story together, like a game, like we were a team, it was... I don't know.

It probably wasn't good, whatever it was. Anything that deludes me into thinking that Bastien and I are anything more than prisoner and prison guard is a bad idea. I just need to remember that.

The rest of the visit passes pleasantly enough. It's only once the door closes behind them and Bastien turns to me that I remember: prisoner and prison guard—right.

"You ready?" he asks.

"And if I'm not?"

Weariness battles frustration on his features. "Let's not do this."

"Fine," I sniff. "We won't."

I turn on my heel and head for the basement. Through the door, down the stairs, and...

"Hold on," he calls.

I look back up the stairs just as he appears at the threshold of the open door. "Yes?"

The reluctant expression on Bastien's face... that is a smile, isn't it? "Thank you. For today."

"It was nothing," I murmur. "I almost had fun."

He looks down at me and I look up at him, and as we do, something passes between us. Like a knot tightening. Pulling us closer and closer, even as we're both flailing against it helplessly.

But then Bastien says, "Have a good night," and it all falls away.

I watch him go without a word. I wait there for a long time. For him to pause, turn back, kiss me how I can see he wants to.

But by the time I whisper, "You too" into the silence, he's long gone.

I walk down the steps, straight to my bed. Peeling up the mattress, I reach beneath and pull out the key. I hold it in the palm of my hand, turn it round and round and round.

The question asks itself: *Is now the time?*

16

BASTIEN

I scowl. Who the fuck knows at what.

Could be the air, how it smells like we're in a fucking fridge. Could be the music, how it's utterly wrong, a jazz that's overly jaunty for my mood.

Could be any of a million other things. My glare wanders the room, picking out every little thing that's grating on my nerves. It settles eventually on my cousins.

That's it, I decide. *They're what's pissing me off.*

The Limonov brothers look like they belong in a cheesy Tijuana nightclub on spring break, the way they're sprawled back in the booth, eyeing around like they're looking for either a fight or a fuck and can't decide which.

I dig the heel of my combat boot back into the booth. Fucking idiots, the pair of them.

Lukyan, in all black, looks like a goth with a stone to grind. Who knows what the fuck Evgeniy was thinking, wearing that bright teal

Hawaiian shirt with the yellow and red hibiscus, like a sun-addled tourist.

"Reports," I growl. I'm down to one-word conversation at the moment. I've wasted more than enough time waiting for them to get drunk enough to stop snapping at each other.

"Morale is not good," Evgeniy says. "The men are scared. After these two latest hits, how they were waiting at us when we arrived—"

"He doesn't need to know shit we know already," Lukyan snaps.

"Correct," I agree.

I already knew wars can be won and lost in a week. That a tide can turn completely in a few days. But seeing it firsthand like this... Fuck.

It wasn't supposed to be like this. Two hits in the last week have gone awry. A routine weapons pickup shouldn't have hit a snag, but it did. We came in with guns, but the Cubans came in with more. They were waiting for us.

"I still say we could retaliate," Lukyan's saying now, spit flying, blue eyes blazing. "Hit them where it hurts. With something they won't soon forget."

"Like what?"

Lukyan's watery eyes settle dejectedly on his drink. His shoulders slacken. "Dunno. But we can't just let them keep hitting us like this."

"We won't." I take a long swig of my whiskey. It's still my first. Nothing beats a clear head. A lesson the Limonovs could stand to learn.

Evgeniy starts to totter his way upright, hand on the back of the booth for support. "Next round..." he slurs.

I shove him back down. "Sit. You've had enough." I shoot a disgusted glare at Lukyan. "You both have."

Lukyan sinks farther down in his seat.

"This is what the Cubans want," I growl at the pair of them. "To demoralize us. Shove our faces into the dirt."

If I could shake both of them by the scruffs of their necks like misbehaving puppies, I would. As it stands, leaning over the table will have to do. "Let them try. We have our own plan. Tomorrow, we have a meeting with my brothers. They'll have some ideas. They've dealt with situations like this before. We turned things around—in New York, Boston. We can do the same here."

Most of that is true. One key point is not. But it has the intended effect: both Limonovs perk up.

Lukyan's side-smile is approving. "You're calling in the big guns, eh?"

He's right. Only not in the way he thinks he is.

"This meeting has to stay secret," I tell them. "Only tell your men that you know for certain you can trust. I'll be texting you the location shortly."

Both brothers nod uneasily. I look at one, I look at the other.

Playing with rats didn't go well for Gavriil and I last time. But I've learned a thing or two since then. And two hits in two locations that only me and the Limonov brothers knew about in advance equals... a rat.

We'll see if what I'm planning tonight works into this, too.

Abruptly, Evgeniy rights himself in his seat, petulant gaze settling on Lukyan. "Where have you been? Half the times I call you, it goes right to voicemail."

"I have to be on call for you, like your fucking puppy dog now?" Lukyan scoffs—although he can't help slinking a nervous side-eye my way.

I say nothing. Do nothing. Really, Evgeniy has just pointed out what I already noticed.

Lukyan has been acting erratic lately. Missed calls, late to meetings. Even the men have said that he seems distracted. Distraction doesn't necessarily mean betrayal, but where there's smoke, there's fire.

"Just saying," Evgeniy says moodily. "We're in a war. Not the time to be leaving your phone off."

"Find it in your heart to forgive me, Mom," Lukyan growls back.

"Evgeniy is right," I growl at him. "I don't care what's distracting you. Whatever it is, sort it out."

Lukyan opens his mouth, then frowns like he's thought better of it and clamps his lips closed. "Roger."

"I still think," Evgeniy says quietly, "that if we had some kind of contingency plan, something to fall back on, just in case—"

"Don't be such a pussy," Lukyan interrupts.

"He's right," I chime in. "Are you talking to the men like that?"

"No," Ev says sullenly.

"You must know the story of Cortés when he came to the New World," I continue quietly. "His armada landed on the shore and he made his men burn the boats behind them. So that they either had to conquer or die."

"So that's it then," Evgeniy says, running a hand over his head. "You'd rather give us a death sentence than lose."

"We aren't there yet."

"And when will we be?" he asks. "When is it time to cut our losses?"

"You really want to do that?"

"No," Evgeniy says with a sigh. "But Jesus, I'm tired of them handing our asses to us."

"Then fix it," I say. "That's your job as lieutenant: to fix problems."

"Not to bitch about how things aren't going our way," Lukyan adds.

"Planning ridiculous revenge attacks is much better, true," Evgeniy retorts sarcastically.

"At least I am trying to make Papa proud," Lukyan snaps. He's on his feet now, unsteady but angry. "You're not even trying."

Evgeniy's gaze lowers. "I never made him proud before, so why would now be any different?"

"Because now, you know it's counting on you," I say.

"What is?"

"Everything," I say with quiet vehemence. "You don't have your father to fall back on anymore. Everything is crumbling. If there was ever a time to make your mark, it's now."

There's something off about Evgeniy's expression. Like he wants to believe me, but can't. Lucky for us, this Bratva doesn't rest on Evgeniy's shoulders alone.

"Or don't," I add. "Just don't screw this up for the rest of us. The men are having a hard-enough time as it is without hearing gloomy shit from their lieutenants."

Lukyan looks pompously pleased. Time to nip that in the bud.

"And you," I say, rounding on him. "Start answering your fucking phone. All the bravado in the world isn't worth shit if you can't execute on it."

He gives me a surly nod, paired with shifty eyes that I almost call him out on. But if Lukyan is the rat, the last thing I want to do is tip him off that I'm on to him.

"That it?" I ask them.

They nod.

"Good." I rise. I have some business to attend to." I leave without telling them what.

That's the thing about a surprise: once you tell someone, it ceases to be much of a surprise anymore. And if either brother is a traitor, then better I keep my next move to myself.

I also don't want their input on my next move. What I'm about to do is risky at best. Lethal at worst. Then again, many of the best plans are.

I drive there. At a red light, I stretch, my arm muscles tense and tired. Part of me wants to skip this. It's been a long, hard day, and it's not getting any shorter or easier anytime soon.

The night is quiet and damp. Calm before the... well, before the who-fucking-knows.

Could be a storm. Could be a squall. Could be nothing.

The only thing certain is that things have gone far enough. I'm not about to let the tide turn against us. I'm not about to let the Cubans and José fucking Correa think they've got us beat for one more second.

As I arrive at my destination, park my car, and get out, my phone goes off.

Seeing who it is, I let it go to voicemail. Evgeniy isn't wrong about what he said: the men are scared. They aren't the only ones.

Just now, that call I turned down—that was my mother. In the past few days, she's called a dozen times and left voicemails every time. Even when no one is saying it, it's there, in the pauses and the careful questions: the Cubans are making a laughingstock out of us.

Not having an official don in charge here, now that Maksi is dead, isn't helping. Only a bunch of lieutenants and underbosses screwing things up.

No more. There isn't a true don? Fine. Then I'll make myself the fucking don.

The bar in front of me is forgettable. Brick and a lit-up sign that reads *LOCO*. Could be any old watering hole—if I wasn't who I am and I didn't know what I know.

But I am who I am—Bastien Nikolaev. And I do know what I know—that the only way to get what you want is to take it.

Inside, the music is some Top 40 shit. It's as busy as you'd expect a popular bar to be. It stinks of the cheap bar on tap and the plate of unfinished fries on the table by the entrance.

I sit at the bar and order a hard drink with a grunt and a point. Then I sip and I sit and I wait.

It's the first thing you learn about this business: you want to live a long time, you stay in your territory. So what I'm doing now, showing my face here? Any Cuban mobster will know what it is—a declaration of war.

That's exactly what I'm counting on.

I sip my drink, and keep my guard up, my gaze straight ahead and confident. It happens gradually: the gazes flitting to me, then sticking, like flies to a trap. I clutch my drink with one hand, while the other stays light and free. My gun is in its holster, thrumming with anticipation.

I'm waiting. Ready.

For the quick swish of movement, the snap. The only warning I may get before a bullet is speeding toward me and it's my turn to fire.

The Cubans aren't averse to public displays of violence. Especially when it serves them well. A dead Nikolaev? That would be worth its weight in gold.

It's likely they may just decide to shoot me in the back of the head and be done with it. Yet, in their own bar, surrounded by their own clientele, the people whose fear and respect they feed off of... they may think that they need to make an example of me.

I'd love to see them try.

Off to my left are some unsuspecting college girls, decked out in candy-colored dresses and glittery tiaras, screeching off-key to whatever shitty song is playing. On my right, a few tables down, I see an ugly guy in a nice suit who looks vaguely familiar. A corrupt local politician, I think.

While the whiskey burns down my throat, I glance into the corners. Into the shadows, which is where the truth always hides.

That's where my enemies are. Who else would be so quiet in the corner, clearly packing? Who else would recognize me on sight and stare me down like they'd like their fist to meet my face?

And when I look into the abyss, I see the abyss looking back at me.

Five pairs of eyes. Mean, slitted eyes, blurred with just enough drink to be dangerous.

Their hands dance on the table. Tattooed. Restless. The hands of violent men.

A sudden and unexpected thought crosses my mind: *How dare they lay those hands on Melissa?* I have to shake it away before it consumes me. But it leaves anger burning in its wake.

One of the men blows me a kiss. Cocky fuck, that one. That'll work. I'm itching to go, and he is the match that will light the fuse.

So I give him the finger.

The five of them are up and lumbering towards me in a flash. They're bigger than I expected. Not that it concerns me, seeing as how I outweigh the largest by fifty pounds and a lifetime of training.

"You got something to say, *cabrón?*" says one with a squeaky voice and steroid-pumped biceps as they circle around my stool.

"I think he was just leaving," rumbles another.

"No," I say, very calmly. "I think I'll have another drink first."

Five pairs of eyebrows arrow downwards in confusion. No one talks to them like this. But then again…

They've never met anyone like me.

While the five morons try to puzzle out what's happening, I punch the closest one in the throat. I feel the crack of his windpipe breaking.

The squeaky one is the first to respond. He raises his fist to bring it down on me like a hammer. Before he gets anywhere close, though, I pluck my whiskey glass off the bar top and smash it across his head. Glass shatters. Blood spurts.

Another Cuban takes the window of opportunity to unload a fist in my gut. I feel the briefest flare of pain. Then that pain turns into anger.

His follow-up punch misses. Mine doesn't.

His nose breaks satisfyingly under my knuckles. He hits the ground hard. The whole building shakes.

Two down, three to go.

A pair of the stragglers approach. They have a reasonable imitation of fighting stances, although I'm guessing it's more from watching UFC fights than from getting their own hands dirty.

But my next move isn't the kind of thing you see on pay-per-view.

I tip the barstool into my hand and whirl it around like a baseball bat. *CRACK-CRACK-CRACK* go three of the legs on the first man's skull.

The second one dives out of the way, but that only sets up what happens next. Still holding the barstool, I bring it down on his torso. He screams as the jagged wood pierces his gut.

That makes one, two, three, four of them. But weren't there...?

Number five takes me down in a chokehold from behind. We collapse to the wood floor, his arms like anacondas across my throat.

Further off, there's voices raised in alarm. Doesn't matter. Only winning does.

This man is strong. But I have one thing he doesn't—the ability to suffer.

I slam my head back into his. A lightning bolt of pain splits my skull immediately, but it has the intended effect. His grip loosens.

I break free, whirl around, and then deliver a trio of punches to the side of his head. The lights in his eyes slacken, dim, and snuff out.

That makes me five for five.

Most of the Cubans are either unconscious or too dazed from blunt force trauma to the head to be of much use. But the one with the barstool stabbing into his stomach is alert enough to remember what I'm about to tell him.

I walk over and crouch at his side. "José is done in this city," I growl as I press down on the barstool enough to make him scream. "Make sure to tell him that, okay, *cabrón?* This is Nikolaev territory now."

The bar has gone dead silent. Looks like the college girls are long gone—although the politician remains planted in place with a dumbfounded expression. He looks rattled, like he doesn't know who to complain to.

"You hear me?" I roar, loud enough so they can all hear. "This is Nikolaev territory now."

No one answers. That's fine—I know they're listening. More importantly, José is listening.

I stand, straighten my shirt, and stride out of the bar. Every inch of me is tingling with purpose and energy. Nothing I like better than a good fight where I'm outnumbered. A hard, nasty brawl where the choice is win or die.

Burn the boats. It's good advice.

17

MELISSA

What to do, what to do? Let's see, I've already…

Talked to Imaginary Mom and Imaginary Kayla.

Listened for Bastien.

Got pissed at myself for listening for Bastien.

Made my bed and remade it, tried and failed to nap, rehid the stupid key about four thousand times.

And now, I'm so bored I could scream.

A song starts forming in my head. Soon enough, the words spill out of me: *"El día que te encontré me enamoré, Tú sabes que yo nunca lo he negado, Con saña me lograste enloquecer…"*

Somewhere above me, a door slams. Footsteps follow—foot stomps, rather.

My heart leaps—it's Bastien.

My heart then drops as the basement door is thrown open with way more force than it ever has been.

Unless... no. They couldn't have found me. Not yet.

I shrink back into the corner. There's no time to hide, no time to—

The next second, Bastien is storming towards me, dressed in gray jeans and a black t-shirt and hair effortlessly tousled to perfection.

Happy warmth buzzes in my abdomen at his nearness. I have just enough time to register his bloodied face and knuckles before his lips slam onto mine.

Whoa. Talk about a hello.

I wrench my lips away and him over with worry. "What happened?"

God, his face, those hands... and that ferocious gleam still in his eyes. The answer is obvious: Bastien has been fighting—but who, and why?

"Business," he says simply.

My hand clasps his as I tip my forehead against his chin. "Tell me you didn't do anything stupid."

"I did what needed to be done."

My breath catches as I rip myself away to eye him. "What does that mean?"

"It means exactly what I said," he growls. "Whatever it takes. To win, to beat the Cubans. If it takes doing something stupid, then I'll do it."

"But you could get yourself killed," I argue. "You've seen what the Cubans are capable of. José is a dangerous man."

Bastien just laughs. "And I'm not?"

He looks so goddamn handsome, even half-crazed like this, that I have to force myself to look away before I do something stupid of my own. "And what would happen to me if you got yourself killed?" I say, crossing my arms over my chest. "Huh? You think your friends would treat me so nice?"

"Always looking out for yourself, aren't you?"

"Someone has to."

That's not it; that's not even half of it. Truth is that I know better than to blurt out what I'm thinking: *I don't want anything to happen to you.*

I don't bother voicing it. I've seen how well trying to be honest and open with him has worked before.

"Anyway," I continue quietly, "even if I was trying to look out for you, you wouldn't listen anyway, would you?"

"That's the pot calling the kettle black."

I roll my eyes. "I'm trying to have a serious conversation."

"I'm not. Come here," he orders.

"No."

"Don't make me tell you again."

"Fuck you," I hiss.

He's on me just as fast as he was the first time. Pressing me against the concrete wall, his mouth a hot slash over mine, his tongue saying in no uncertain terms, *You belong to me, princess.*

I sigh into him. What else can I do?

He kisses me hard, and he kisses me his. I can feel the kiss travel through my entire body, top to bottom. I lose myself in it.

His hands roam all across me, over and under my clothes. Up, above my bare hips and further, along my rib cage, snagging on my bra and then diving beneath it to tweak my nipples savagely enough to make me sag in his arms.

"Oh," I groan.

Another hand drags down until he slips inside me. I can hardly stand. Can hardly think. Already, I'm near the edge, collapsed onto him. Lost, so lost in it, that I could just...

"Oh no, princess," he snarls in my ear. "You're going to have to wait to come this time."

He takes his fingers out of me and hurls me unceremoniously onto the bed. The breath rushes from my lungs when I land, but before I can inhale again, he's on top of me. His massive body pins me down. I'm so wet I can hardly stand it.

Leaning away, Bastien makes quick work of ripping my panties down my legs in one tangled mess. He discards them over his shoulder without a care.

I lean up to reach for him, but his eyes flare and he presses me right back into the mattress with one huge hand on my throat.

"Stay right there," he commands. "I want to drink you in."

He pauses above me, huge and irresistible, and does exactly that. Rakes over me with eyes like a touch. I'm more naked than naked, more exposed than exposed. I'm his in every way that matters.

His eyes track down my body to my wetness, then back up to meet mine. His gaze afire. "Beautiful," he murmurs. "Fucking beautiful."

Then he's unzipping his pants and pulling out his dick and sliding into me without hesitation. No teasing this time. No making me wait. Just filling me to the hilt and breathing into my face. I drink him in like he did to me, because he's so fucking beautiful I want to cry.

And what he's doing to me is every bit as gorgeous. Making me come apart in his arms.

He starts to thrust into me slowly. I cling to his arms where they're planted on either side of me, desperate for something solid and real.

Time twists and contorts. I don't know if he's been fucking me for a minute or an hour. His hugeness fills me all the way. I never knew what it was before. To be filled. Dominated. Owned.

"Bastien," I moan.

"Melissa," he growls right back.

Our eyes meet.

His eyes aren't just brown; there are a dozen different shades in there. Honey, mocha, black, flecks of gold... And the look in them is—well, can he actually be thinking what I am?

That: him and me, us, we're perfect for each other. Made for each other. That this is the best sex I've ever had or ever will have. That—

Bastien looks away.

And all I can do to that is hiss, *"No."*

I grab his face and turn his gaze back to me. He can't avoid this anymore. Can't deny it.

He needs to look me in the eyes and admit what he feels.

We peak right then, and as my orgasm crashes over me and his does the same to him, I can see it in his eyes that he knows how right this is.

The transition to the aftermath happens gradually. My breath and my limbs are still tangled with his. His powerful arms stay rooted around me. The sheet is a knot around our ankles. His heart throbs slowly against my cheek. Slow and inexorable.

I want him to talk first, to say something. But I know he won't, so I do. "So... that just happened."

"Yes."

"That's all you have to say?"

He does a one-shouldered shrug. "What else am I supposed to say?"

"Say what you think! Like, I think that was amazing," I say frankly.

Screw playing it safe. I'm tired of trying to protect myself. Or maybe it's just the after-pleasure that's still swirling in me, clouding my thoughts. Who knows? I might regret all this before I'm even finished saying it.

"Yeah," is all Bastien says.

I turn around so that my chin is resting on his rock-hard chest. Eyeing him makes my frustration dissipate. There's something about him... his gaze has a darkness to it I can't place.

Different than usual. Deeper, more frightening.

"What is it?" I ask.

"Nothing." He looks away.

"Bastien."

God, talking to this man is like pulling teeth sometimes. Maybe even less satisfying: at least you know what you're getting when pulling teeth.

He sighs. "About the other day, what you were telling me about the Cubans..." His glance slants back over to me. "What did they do to you and your mother?"

Oh.

Suddenly, I'm the one looking away, letting silence be the response.

The question morphs and splinters into every possible configuration: *What did they do to you, what did they do to your mom, what did they do to you and your mom, what did* you *do to your mom*—twisting, twisting...

I force my involuntarily clenched fists open. "It doesn't matter," I say, wishing it were so.

"Yes," he argues. "It does."

"I shouldn't have even told you that," I mutter on an exhale. "There are so many things..."

"So many things what?" he asks.

I sit up and hug my legs to my chest, staring into the corner. As if, if I can just outwait his question for long enough, it will disappear, along with everything it's referring to.

"So many things you don't know," I finish in a soft murmur.

My heart starts to thud, knowing what I'm thinking of doing—telling him what I haven't even dared to think about myself, lest he somehow guess at it, see it in my eyes.

Bastien doesn't say anything. That just makes it worse. Leaves more room for my thoughts to war.

You have to tell him.

I can't tell him.

You have to.

I can't.

Over and over again, two voices screaming at each other with no resolution in sight.

"Did they touch you?" he snarls. I feel his tension like a shift in the air. Like the first cold breeze of an incoming storm.

"No. I mean, they tried. But José wouldn't let them. Wanted to keep us club girls 'pure,' as he called it, the scumbag control freak. He figured that if we wouldn't sleep with anyone, then the men would pay more to see us take off our clothes. He made good money, at any rate, so who knows, maybe he was right."

Bastien's gaze goes serious. "Are you saying...?"

I laugh. "God, no. I'm no virgin. Kayla and I found ways to cover for each other for the few times we found guys who weren't Cuban and actually decent. Not that it ever lasted long. When José found out, he had us beaten and the guys scared off. We didn't try anything after that."

"Fucking José," Bastien mutters.

I can't help laughing. "That's exactly what Kayla and I used to say. It was our 'Jesus Christ', our swear word. When we were at the club, we'd call it FJ for short. Fucking José."

"It's not funny," Bastien asserts. "That man needs to be put down."

That fire in his eyes... like mistreating *me* was the worst crime a Cuban mob boss could commit. It does... *things...* to me.

"Just see that you're not the one to do it, okay?" I plead.

"Why not?"

I just shake my head. "It's too risky. José is crazy."

Bastien scowls. "I won't ask my men to do anything I'm not willing to do. Not how I lead. If anyone's going to do it, it's going to be me."

"That sounds all nice and brave. But you won't win your war if you're dead."

"And I won't win it while José is still alive."

"Believe me, Bastien," I tell him. "If anyone wants José dead, it's me. The number of times he made me feel lower than dirt... How he actually *chuckled* when he watched Kayla and I being beaten until we were crying. What he had me do to my mother..." I force out a shuddering exhale. "But the man is too well-protected, too smart. He's always one step ahead."

"Are you doubting me, *kotyonok*?"

"I'm doubting everyone," I correct. "The man's like a cockroach. He's gonna live forever."

"Not if I have anything to say about it."

God, he really isn't hearing me. I have to—but no, I can't. I can't tell him *that*.

I'll just have to convince him some other way.

"Bastien, listen to me," I say, taking his hand and giving it a squeeze. "José is always a step ahead. Always."

"Unfortunately for him, I'm three steps past that."

He wraps his arms around me and I sigh into it. It would be so easy to just sit here and let the subject go. To just enjoy the rest of the time I have with Bastien.

But I can't.

I can see it now. If I don't tell Bastien what I know, if I don't tell him the whole, unfiltered truth about this, then he's going to get himself killed. He's going to walk in blind when he tries to face off with José, and then he won't stand a chance.

I can't have that.

I can't lose him.

Even if, with what I'm about to tell him, I might lose him anyway.

I pull away. "There's something I have to tell you."

"What is it?" he says.

His face hasn't changed yet. I take a breath and memorize it as it is now—because God knows if I'll ever see it this way again. The affection in his eyes. Trust, I think. Maybe even love. Or something that could grow into love.

I make sure to save it all for the dark moments that are right around the corner. Just like I saved Mama's voice to get me through the nightmares, I'm saving Bastien's face to get me through his hatred.

Because what I'm about to say is going to ruin everything.

I look away at the last second. It's cowardly, but I don't want to see that trust and hope shatter in his eyes. I don't want to see it burned with violence.

So, facing the wall, I take a deep breath and say, "They sent me here to spy on you."

18

BASTIEN

Rage ratchets through me like a gasoline fire. I'm off the bed immediately and before I can even think to stop myself, I'm punching the solid concrete wall.

It's instant agony. But even the pain bolting through my knuckles pales in comparison to how it feels to have my heart ripped out of my chest.

They sent me here to spy on you.

And of all things she could've said, that was one I honestly had stopped expecting. What does that make me? A deluded fool. A blindsided fucking idiot.

I chose to keep this pretty snake under my roof.

I chose to sleep with her, to talk to her.

I chose to *trust* her.

Now, it's all come back to bite me in the ass. And it's my own goddamn fault.

"Bastien," she says, far away.

I don't turn back to face her. Part of me fears that if I look Melissa in the eye right now, I'll kill her.

"Bastien," she says, louder now, more pleading.

My breath is slow and measured. A counterbalance against the anger surging in my chest. *Keep control,* Father taught. *The man who maintains his control in the heat of battle is the man who emerges victorious.*

So I breathe, and breathe, and breathe.

It doesn't help.

"Bastien," she repeats, clutching for me. "Listen, what I mean is that I'm *supposed* to be spying for them."

More words. More lies. This is all a game to her. Maybe that's all it has been from the start.

I know what she wants. She wants me to look at her until I give into those pretty green eyes with their pretty sadness. She wants me to lose myself in them, in her, until I forget and slip up again.

Too bad I don't make the same mistake twice.

"You won't even look at me?" she asks.

I don't speak, don't turn.

"I'm sorry, Bastien," she says softly. "Truly, I… Here, I'll tell you it. All of it."

If she expects a response, she's not getting any. I'm hardly listening, as it is. Not that my thoughts are more productive. Circling back, back to the same thing, always circling back: *I've been a fool.*

It bears remembering, though: whatever she says, whatever she "explains," is not to be trusted.

She plows ahead anyway, voice quiet and sad. "I was at the club on purpose that night you came. Me and Antonia. José already knew about how you Nikolaevs don't kill women—all the Cubans have a good chuckle about it from time to time. They think it's very prude of you. Anyway, he knew you were coming and what he wanted was someone to get to you. He wanted an excuse to get rid of El Palacio, anyway. The old place was a dump and he wanted the insurance money out of it."

My jaws clench with how much sense this is making. All the low-level nobodies at the club. How easy it was for us to go in, guns blazing. The pathetic security at the door.

José was fine with sacrificing all of it. Just wrote it off as the cost of doing business.

It wasn't part of our plan—it was part of *his*.

"Anyway, it was one of our jobs—me or Antonia—to get close to you," she's saying now. "Since she got killed in the gunfight, it was left to me. My job was to get as close as I could, and get whatever information I could. Even kill you if I got the chance. Later, they'd 'rescue' me and I'd tell them everything I knew."

The obviousness of this is striking. The sort of shit I normally would've seen a mile away. For fuck's sake, he pulled the wool over my eyes so easily.

"So," I say slowly, "this has all been part of the plan."

"I'm sorry," she says. Her hands are slack at her sides, not knowing what to do now that she's seen how useless clutching at me is. "I can't tell you how sorry I am. I didn't want to do it. I told José I wouldn't. But he stopped by late one night with some thugs, and he mentioned how easily Kayla and I could have a little 'accident,' and I knew that I had to. He would've killed me otherwise. Kayla, too."

"What makes you think that I won't, now that I know the truth?"

Out of the corner of my eye, I see her hang her head. "You won't. I'd understand if you do, but I don't think you will."

"No?" I whirl on her, fist raising high in the air, ready to come down on her like Judgment Day.

I want her to cry out, beg, back away. But she only swallows. She doesn't even flinch.

"I know what you must think of me," she says quietly. "But please, Bastien, you have to believe that I never wanted to do this. I've been fighting against it for days now."

"Just stop," I say, turning away and shaking my head. "Stop fucking talking."

"No, I won't," she says. She reaches out to grasp for me, saying. "Bastien, please—"

I knock her hand away, lunge forward, and grab her by the throat.

I could end her now, so easily. But then she looks at me with nothing but sorrow in those emerald eyes and I can't bring myself to do it.

So I freeze with Melissa at arm's length. Too close and too far away at the same time.

"Bastien, you have to listen to me," she pleads. "I never wanted this, but it happened. All this is real. You and me, it's real. What I feel for you is real."

I don't say anything.

It's all there on her face: that she means it, that she's tormented by it, that she doesn't realize yet that it's all too late.

She draws herself up as she speaks some more. "For the past decade, I've been a plaything of the Cubans. I wear what they want, eat what they want, dance where they want. I've worked and lived and breathed at their beck and call for almost half my life now. Some days, I can't even remember what it was like, living with my parents. Maybe I'm just overdoing how happy I was in our colorful home to make up for my drab present. They've stolen everything from me, everything. They're even stealing my memory now. There are no pictures of my parents left. Any extended family thinks I died all those years ago." Her head falls and her voice shrinks, like she's talking to herself as much as me. "I've gone through the motions for so long that I forgot what it was like to be free. But with you... even if I'm still locked up in this basement, I know it's crazy, but I feel freer than I ever have. Almost like I might actually have a future, and it might even be a good one I would like. And Bastien, I—"

Pink cheeks flush, green eyes bright, her gaze catches mine.

But my anger isn't satisfied. Who says this isn't just part of the plan, the part that she hasn't told me about? The last time someone expects to be betrayed is right after you've confessed that you've already done it.

Fuck that. I don't make the same mistake twice.

No matter how tempting the mistake is.

"You could've told them as soon as you got your hands on that phone. Why didn't you?"

"Because I hate them," she whispers bitterly. "And I'm not as broken as they think I am."

There's a ferocity in the narrows of her teared eyes that goes tender when she turns my face so I'm looking at her. "And, Bastien, I think I'm starting to fall for you."

I swallow, drawing away. Ripping my gaze off her is like tearing a bandage off an open wound.

I settle onto the bare mattress. I return my gaze to the crack in the wall where I punched it. It'll have to be filled at some point. I'll need to hire a mason, or buy concrete mix and do it myself.

I know I'm only thinking about this to avoid thinking about her. It's easier to focus on things I can do. Simple, straightforward work—

that's what I've always been best at. *Bastien, break this. Bastien, kill this.* There's comfort in action.

But this? This crack cannot simply be filled.

I lift my bloodied hand and study it. What a fucking day.

Still, there's questions that need answers. Even if they just delay the inevitable moment when I leave. When I close that door and never look back.

"What happened the night your mother died?" I ask. "If that was even the truth."

Melissa settles beside me. Not close enough to touch, not far enough to ignore.

"I never lied to you. I just didn't tell you that I was supposed to be spying. Believe me, I wish the part about Mama was a lie. God, how I wish."

"Tell the story, Melissa."

"It was a Tuesday," she recounts dully. "I remember because it was the night we always went to the Cuban club. This Tuesday, we argued about it, Mama and me. She wanted me to stay home and study for school the next day. I wanted to go in and sing. That never got old to me. I could sing for three hours straight, even longer sometimes, so much that I'd barely be able to talk until the next week, when I'd do it all again."

She's looking at my bloodied hand in my lap like it's the saddest thing she's ever seen.

"So," she continues, "I wanted to go and she didn't. We yelled at each other. I told her that she was the worst mother ever, said all sorts of horrible things. The kind of things I would've apologized for by the next day. Only, I never got the chance."

I wince and close my eyes. I've seen enough death to know where this story is going.

Melissa takes a breath. "Mama gave in, in the end. She and Papa had been fighting more—something to do with Papa's work, was all I knew– and she'd seen the stress it was putting on me. So we went in, the three of us. Mama and me were singing when it happened. I'll never forget the song. *Te regalo mi cintura... Y mis labios para cuando quieras besar...*"

Her eyes close as a single shuddering breath escapes her lips. And when they open again, they're staring lifelessly ahead.

"The men came so fast. Six of them," she says. "While Mama and I were singing. They took Papa. He tried to joke with them at first. When he saw that it was real, he struggled and cried out for help. No one helped. No one would even look. We tried to run after them, save him, but others held us back. Turned out he was an informant and he'd been caught. Anyway, I never saw him again. The whispers said they took him offshore in a boat and sank his body to the bottom of the ocean. I'll never know for certain. Mama and me, they took us down to the basement. José was so mad. He'd been having problems with snitches, so he took Papa to send a message. Mama and I, what he did to us? That was the message. And it worked. No one dares snitch on José Correa anymore."

The silence in the room is deafening. I can hear my own heartbeat pounding in my ears. *Ba-boom. Ba-boom.*

"He left us down there for a few days. No food, no water. Then, when we were sleeping, they came to finish what they started." Her eyes are wide and unseeing, like she's in a trance. "They strung Mama up to the ceiling. She was screaming and crying and begging for them to have mercy, to please, please, please let me go. She didn't ask for anything for herself, not even once. She just wanted them to keep me out of it. And then they shoved me in front of her and pressed the gun in my hands, with the nozzle pointed right at her. They grabbed me so

19

BASTIEN

Tonight will tell who the rat is—and who needs to be put down like one.

Two locations. Two plans. I'm hiding out at the location where I told Lukyan to meet me, with my best men at my side.

Somewhere in the dank dark alongside me, Vlad sneezes. He's already mouthing *Sorry* by the time my glare finds him.

He should know better. The whole point of being under the goddamn floorboards in this place was to avoid notice.

It's a little harder when every inhale down here is more dust than oxygen. Ten of us are crammed sardine-tight, sweating and antsy for the violence that's about to explode.

Up above, we have one of our boys with a bulletproof vest under his suit posing as the maître d'. We have the lights on and the tables set. We have nice, wholesome jazz playing.

But the only things our guests will be eating are bullets.

I check my phone. ***All good here, boss,*** Joro's message says.

He's at the other restaurant—Winchester's—that I told Evgeniy was the location of the real meeting. I doubt he will see any action, which I'm sure is just fine with him. The situation over there looks the same so far, though: ten of my men in the kitchen, all armed to the teeth.

But I feel it in my gut: here is where the action will be.

Lukyan is not an unpredictable man, and yet, lately, he has been acting just that. Unpredictable. Unnerved. Unreliable. His shifty eyes, unexplained absences. Leaving his phone off. All signs point to him being our rat, even if he has outwardly been the most vehement in his support of the Bratva and continuing his father's legacy.

If I've learned anything in recent days, though, it's this: we can never really know people, no matter how close we think we are.

That was the mistake I made with Melissa. Thinking I knew her.

My scowl deepens. She doesn't matter now. Better not to think of her at all. And yet there she is in my mind's eye. Her eyes. Her voice.

It's only been two fucking days, but there's an ache in my chest like a splinter I can't remove.

I glance down at my watch. Should only be a few more minutes now. Down in the corner, barely visible, a spider has caught an unsuspecting fly. It's doing the slow and methodical work of wrapping it in its web, wrapping it to its death.

Poignant.

Up above, I can hear the door open. The maître d says his predetermined greeting.

Go time.

But once I'm out of the cellar and peering around the corner, all I see is Lukyan accompanied by two of his men. No army of Cubans swarming in to cut my throat.

He goes to sit at the long table by the back wall that the maître d'
indicates. We picked it for how exposed it is to our hiding place.

I wait, turning with a finger to my lips to my men. We all stand still.
Waiting. Watching.

Lukyan picks up his phone and starts texting something. My frown
deepens. Maybe he's waiting to confirm that we're here first before he
gives the Cubans the word?

I call up the lookout I have stationed outside. "Any movement?"

"Nothing Cuban, boss," Anton says. "Just Lukyan and his men a few
minutes ago."

Fuck. No one's coming. No Cubans.

Lukyan isn't the rat.

I was wrong.

I gesture to my men to leave through the back entrance, a couple of
doors that swing quietly on oiled hinges. I signal for all but two of
them to disperse, taking most of my heavy weaponry with them. Then
my little trio strides into the restaurant through the proper front
door.

Despite the circumstances, as I walk in, my gaze is drawn to the
beautifully frescoed walls. *A colorful home in a drab existence...* Melissa's
words, of course, stuck in my head like an earworm melody.

As I approach, Lukyan rises, still holding the menu. "You got my text?
What's going on?"

"The dinner has been canceled," I tell him.

"Canceled," he repeats. And, once again, the man looks nervous. Like I
might know something he doesn't want to.

For fuck's sake—if the man isn't a rat, then what is he?

"There was never any dinner," I growl. "I'll explain in the car."

I still haven't received word about what is or isn't happening at Evgeniy's location, but it has to be him. It can only be him.

"You don't trust me," Lukyan says, looking hurt. "You've done this as punishment."

I look at him, unblinking. "Have you done something that merits punishment?"

When he doesn't answer, I continue, "If I wanted to punish you, believe me cousin, I wouldn't waste my time coming up with a stupid fake dinner. As for trust..." Lukyan has backed behind his chair as I continue speaking, as though subconsciously wanting a shield. "Trust is earned, cousin. And thus far, the way you've been acting has not inspired trust. Quite the opposite, in fact."

Just then, my phone goes off. "Yeah?" I say, picking up.

"The Cubans are here!" roars Joro. "There's a lot and they're already firing—shit!" Gunfire sounds in the background of the call before he hangs up abruptly.

"Let's go," I tell Lukyan. I'm already striding to the door. "The Cubans are attacking the Winchester."

On the ride there in the car, I look Lukyan over. There's the possibility that both brothers are rats, and that right now, I'm taking one to join forces with the other. There are more questions that need answering.

I take out my gun, hold it casually in my lap. "Now, you're going to tell me what's going on."

Lukyan's eyes bulge.

I study him. The dark circles under his eyes, the twitchy posture of his hands. "Talk, *mudak.*"

"Nothing!" he bleats. "Nothing."

"You're not helping the Cubans?"

"What? No!" he says, face reddening as his gaze sneaks to my gun—is it fear talking? Or the truth? "How could you even for a second think—"

"You haven't been answering your phone," I say. "You look more shit every time I see you. You've been acting erratic. Why?"

Lukyan looks impossibly nervous. "You're not going to like it."

"I already don't like it."

"No, I mean, you're really not going to—"

"Lukyan," I spit, "I'm not a patient man. And there's not much time."

"I'm sorry, I just—"

"I don't care. If I can't trust you, then I'm locking you in this car with either a man to guard you or a bullet in your head. You want that?"

There's always the possibility that Lukyan lies now, to save his skin. But whatever my cousin is, he's not a good liar.

"I won't ask again."

His answer comes out on a sigh. "It's this girl. A Cuban girl."

I close my eyes. Jesus fucking Christ.

"I haven't been telling her anything," he continues, "but for fuck's sake, Bastien, I'm obsessed. Every day I get this compulsive need to see her. I keep rescheduling my whole fucking life just to fit her in it." He shakes his head in disbelief. "I don't know how it happened. Sure as hell don't know how to control it. It's messing with my head. I mean, *blyat'*, she's a Cuban! Not involved in anything, as far as I know, but still. Who really knows?"

"How long?" I ask him.

"A few weeks," Lukyan admits. "I'm sorry, Bastien, I really am. I had no idea who she was until it was too late, and now... I can't get enough of her." He directs his gaze and stooped shoulders to the window. "I don't expect you to understand. What it's like when you've got someone in your bones."

My jaw clenches. Oh, I know. All too fucking well. Even now, as we're racing towards a life-and-death gunfight and I'm interrogating my cousin, *she* still pops into my head.

"So, about this fight," Lukyan says. "If you still don't trust me…"

"I don't," I say flat-out. "Not after what you've let get in the way of work."

His head hangs. I reach out to put a hand on his shoulder. "But I do trust you to hold a gun and know where to point it. We're going to need all the help we can get at this fight we're heading into. Can I count on you for that?"

Lukyan's head shoots up, eyes fiery with excitement. "Yes! Fuck yes! Let's show these Cuban *pridurki* what happens when they try to fuck with the Bratva."

"Good. Evgeniy's the rat," I explain. "That was Joro on the phone. He says the Cubans showed up at the other location."

Lukyan doesn't look quite as stunned as I thought he would. "My own fucking brother."

"He will pay for what he's done," I promise.

Lukyan looks away, although his head moves in what looks like a nod. "Do what you have to do. My brother is dead to me already."

"We should've cut him loose weeks ago, maybe even months," I say. "He isn't meant for this life."

Lukyan shakes his head, eyes wide in disbelief. "I still don't understand it. Why help the Cubans? After what they did to Papa…"

"Guess we're about to find out."

"Fucking hell. He would be so ashamed." He breathes hard, shakily. "One son in love with a Cuban, the other in bed with them."

I put a steadying hand on his shoulder. "We can make this right," I tell him. "We are going to put these Cubans down. We are going to show them who really owns Miami. We are going to kill every last one of them."

Lukyan takes one last, ragged, deep breath, then lifts his head to face me, his gaze hard. "Yes, cousin. We will."

We pull up outside the restaurant just then. As soon as the door opens, I can hear the crack of bullets in the starless night.

The building that houses Winchester's is one giant, white-stuccoed wave: all circular curves, no sharp corners. From within, I hear more of the *pop-pop-pop* of desperate men trading fire.

The gunfire could be anyone's, but if my men are still roughly where they started, then I should try entering from the back doors.

"This way."

As we hurry down the alley to the rear entrance, it soon becomes clear why we could hear the bullets from so far away: the fight has been brought outside, into the parking lot.

I pause at the corner and survey the scene.

Cubans hold the spots closest to the building, ducked behind a bullet-ridden black Impala. No man's land is in the center. I see some of our guys' corpses splayed off to the side, halfway to a flaming car.

Further on are our surviving men, ducked behind cars that look just as wrecked as the Cuban's shield. At just a glance, it's obvious that the Cubans are at an advantage.

More men and a better spot, protected by the restaurant at the back and some dumpsters at the side. If they send some men to double back and attack ours from another direction, we're fucked.

Which means we better get over there—and fast.

No time for a better plan then "shoot and run like hell until we join the others."

I gesture to Lukyan and the men who followed us here from the other location, then take off, all of us spraying bullets at the Cubans as we race to join the others and take cover behind the van.

Stunned by the unexpected gunfire, the Cubans react to us too late. They hardly get a shot in before we're ducked behind the van with the others.

I turn to Joro. His matted beard is glistening with sweat and blood. "How bad is it?"

"Not good," he says, breathing hard. "Three of ours dead, and a couple wounded. A couple of others are trapped behind that burning car over there."

"Fucking Evgeniy," Lukyan swears.

I ignore him. Now is not the time for blame. Nor rage.

It's time to plan. Fast and effective and deadly.

More bullets thunk into the metal of the van in front of us. I dive around the side to trade gunfire with some of the more trigger-happy Cubans.

I hear a shout, then a renewed volley of return fire. I duck just in time, as a bullet whizzes right above where I was a quarter-second ago.

"Close shave," Lukyan hisses from beside me. He's pressed flat on the ground, eyes maniacal, holding his own gun with a twisted smile. He squeezes off a clip, taking down one or two Cubans, then reloads with a menacing growl.

I make eye contact with Joro and gesture towards the flaming car. "We have to help the others over there."

He shakes his head. "How do you think the two others died?"

I peer over in that direction. The men hunkered down over there have minutes, if that, before the thing explodes and roasts them alive. "If we don't act, they'll die, too."

My gaze travels the long distance I'll have to run, out in the fucking open, to make it there.

It's a long shot, but I've survived worse.

I turn to Lukyan, who, following my gaze, is already shaking his head furiously. "Bastien. No. You can't. It's too risky and—"

"I didn't ask for your input. Just fucking cover me," I tell him.

And then I'm on my feet and sprinting as fast as I can for the flaming car. Bullets crack right after and ahead of me. One almost grazes my leg.

I'm ten yards away, five, two, and then I dive behind the flaming car. Out of the frying pan and into the literal fire.

It's hot here. The flames are loud, and there's a nasty sound coming from the car, a crunching, keening wail that says danger is looming. An engine about to burst and rain hellfire over all of us camped out back here.

The two Bratva soldiers gape at me like I'm a mirage. "We've got to get out of here!" I roar at them.

"But they'll shoot us!" one protests. Yuri, I think his name is.

"No," I snarl, hauling them to their feet. "I'll cover you both. Now go!"

I shove the first out from behind the vehicle. The crack of bullets gets him moving. I push the second ahead of me, then run after them, unloading shot after shot at the pockmarked Impala that's protecting our enemies.

I hit one in the hand and smile grimly as he drops out of sight, screaming Spanish curses. I hit the next one in the head.

But just as we make it back behind our van, I hear something that doesn't fit: a car engine revving.

Fuck.

"They're trying to escape!" Lukyan yells.

We throw open the van and jump in as the Cubans' getaway car races off. But turning the key in the ignition produces only a sad sputtering.

Of fucking course. This piece of shit has done its last turn of the wheel.

"Over here!" I yell, and we run back to the front, for the truck that Lukyan and I took here.

Getting in the driver's seat, I hit the gas and speed after the Cubans. Careening down the streets, with my foot all the way down on the gas, weaving around cars, on the road that eventually leads to the highway, I find them.

I weave around the other cars and settle right beside my prey. I line up, waiting for my chance.

Waiting…

Waiting…

Now.

I throw my van all the way to the left, pinning theirs against the cement divider. Both vehicles screech to a stop. I smash out my window with an elbow, stick my gun through the opening, and prepare to send death pouring into the other car—

And then I stop.

Evgeniy looks back at me from the passenger's seat. He's gunless, helpless. His eyes have doom written in them.

"Why?" I ask him.

"I was never cut out for this life," he whispers over the sound of metal groaning. "They gave me enough money to start a new one."

He could still lift a gun and take a last-ditch shot at me. But he doesn't.

I know what I have to do.

So I pull the trigger and end his miserable life.

My men follow suit until there's no way anything is left alive in that car. Then it's time to go, leaving my dead cousin and a half dozen of our enemies there to rot until the police find them.

I speed away and keep on speeding, even if there's no one to chase now and no one on our trail.

"Holy shit," Lukyan says after a few minutes of silence. In his voice is everything: disgust, shock, sadness. The same feelings that I've put away for later, for long after this.

When I must face what I've done.

20

MELISSA

I have the key in my hand when the basement door opens.

I've been sitting on the mattress for hours turning it over and over between my fingers, going back and forth in my head like a schoolgirl plucking petals off a daisy.

He loves me.

He loves me not.

He loves me.

He loves me not.

Unsurprisingly, I haven't made up my mind.

When he steps off the bottom stair, I stand up from the bed. He looks ragged, weary, but at the core of him is that same nobility that he always has. His shoulders are as powerful as ever, his face as haunted.

As I look at Bastien and try not to look at him at the same time, it's clear that the lie I've spent two days telling myself is complete and utter bullshit.

I don't feel anything for him? Wrong. So, so fucking wrong.

I feel so many things for him that I'm liable to explode at any minute. It's a physical sensation, a fluttery crash of a feeling somewhere deep inside that doesn't have a name.

What could he be here to say? That I'm forgiven? That I'm condemned? It could be either one and I wouldn't be surprised.

"You need anything?" is all he says.

I swallow hard. "I was thinking a hot tub would be nice. Or even a private jet. Though I'd settle for a Lamborghini."

"Hm. I'll look into it."

Nothing in his demeanor says he's in a joking mood. But something in my chest feels like it shifts ever-so-slightly to the left, and I can finally breathe again for the first time in days.

"And while you're at it, could you have the Lamborghini in gold and emblazoned with a rhinestone 'M'? I've always wanted that."

Bastien shakes his head "A girl imprisoned by Cubans pretty much all of her adult life, and what's been on her mind is private jets and luxury cars? I don't think that's what you want."

"You think you know me, do you?"

"No. Before, maybe I thought that. Now...?" His eyes narrow. "Well, it doesn't matter now."

I cross my arms over my chest. "That's what you came down here to say?"

"No," he sighs. "Actually, I came down here to ask you what your dreams are."

"Very funny. Har-de-har-har. A real knee slapper."

He blinks slowly. "It wasn't a joke."

"My dreams? Get out of here. What is this, some kind of word trap?"

"It's a question, Melissa," he says quietly. "Answer it."

"I didn't dream of a single thing for ten years. I never expected to get out."

Bastien takes one slow step toward me. His scent hits me like a tidal wave. I feel weak in the knees, suddenly, unsettled everywhere from head to toe.

"Bullshit," he whispers. He's so big, consuming all of the space in front of me. All of the space inside me, too. "Tell me what you dreamed."

I look straight into his chest because meeting his eyes might ruin me. "Well... sometimes, when it was late at night and I couldn't sleep... when it was one of those shit days at the club I couldn't take, with slimy guys who treated me like I was trash that belonged to them... I'd imagine this life. This life that wasn't mine, that I never really ever felt like could be mine, and yet, maybe... I'd imagine my own room. That's it. Just a room that was mine with a door that could lock. Nothing so simple ever seemed so hard."

I raise my gaze to his, though it's one of the hardest things I've ever done. "Is that what you want to hear?"

He tilts his head to the side. "Do you want to know what I dream?"

I nod shakily, not trusting my voice.

"Nothing. Not a damn thing for my whole entire life... until I met you."

My breath catches in my throat. Everything else fades away until all there is is *him*, gazing down at me with a look I still can't decipher.

"And then I met you, Melissa, and I started to dream. I dreamed so many things, I don't even know the words for them. But you were in all of them. Every single fucking one."

"What happened tonight?" I whisper. "What changed?"

"It was just business."

"Bastien."

"A lot of business," he admits. "We dealt a big blow to the Cubans yesterday. And now, the Bratva wants a change."

My greatest fear escapes my lips before I can even consider how plausible it is. "You're leaving?"

"No," he says. "They want me to become the don here. Just like my brother Dmitry is for New York, and Gavriil for Boston."

My heart thumps hard against my ribs. "What do you want to do?" I ask him in a quivering croak.

He looks at me, then away. God, he has such a beautiful profile. I could sing a song just about the proud jut of his chin, the high, noble slice of his nose.

He stands there, and he doesn't look at me, and he doesn't answer me.

I say again, "What do you want, Bastien?"

"Right this second?" he says, turning his gaze back to me. "I want to hear you sing."

"Don't change the subject," I snap.

"I'm not."

"You can't afford my fee, anyway. Focus, Bastien. Answer the question. *Tell me what you want.*"

There's a long pause while he stares at the crack he left in the wall. Maybe broken things can be mended, if he's willing to try.

"What I want," he says at last in a slow rasp, "is to be able to trust you again. To forget about the past and try for something in the here and now. What I want is you. Here and now. With me."

He looks down at me from all those miles up above. The biggest man I've ever known in every way that matters. The strongest. The bravest. The kindest, even if he doesn't know it. The most merciful. The most loving.

The most mine.

"You can trust me, Bastien," I whisper to him.

He nods. "I know."

21

MELISSA

"Do I get to find out where you're taking me?" I ask as he guides me up the staircase.

"It's a surprise," he says simply. "You'll find out soon enough."

We go up the wooden stairs to the second floor, down the hallway as wide as my old apartment was, and through an ornate gold-knobbed door I've never been through.

And then, there it is: a room.

A room decked out with gorgeously carved furniture, beautiful silk sheets, and a gorgeous view of the ocean in the distance.

I round on him, tears coming to my eyes. "This... it isn't...?"

"The art prints are on their way."

"Bastien," I say. "This isn't—"

"It is." He nods. "All yours."

I stand there for a few seconds, taking it all in. Every little detail. The crisp plane of the ivory bedsheets. The warm goldenrod paint on the walls. The frill of crimson along the bottom edge of the lampshade.

Mine. Even in my head, using that word for this place doesn't seem to fit.

A room of my own.

All I ever wanted.

I sneak a glance behind us. Bastien sees it and winks. "The door locks."

Tears come to my eyes. He has no idea what those three words mean.

The door locks—this place really is mine. I can stay here and choose when I come, when I go. I have the power. I have the freedom.

This place is mine, my door locks, and I am finally, truly free.

He can see me struggling to find words. "If we're going to be together," he says, "I want it on your terms. I want you, but I want you free. No other way."

Of all the possible things I could respond to that with, I choose the absolute worst: I laugh.

Bastien's gaze darkens.

"I'm sorry!" I say, giddy as a little girl. "I just—I'll never be fully free, not really. Not when I care for you how I do. That's all I meant."

Something else occurs to me suddenly. "Wait—so we won't be sleeping in the same room?"

He arches an eyebrow. "You'd never sleep."

"Uh-oh. Are you a snorer?"

"No. I just wouldn't be able to keep my hands off you."

I blush hard, then look up at him through my eyelashes. "You're doing pretty good at that right now, though."

He smirks. "Now that you mention it…"

Next thing I know is his lips on mine, his tongue in my mouth. Really, everything else was just leading up to this. Avoiding this, trying to deny this. This *us*-ness, this perfection that happens when we are together.

Him and me, our bodies making sense of what our minds can't.

We kiss our way to the bed and he takes me the way he always does: like he'll never get to do it again. And I give myself to him in every way I possibly can.

Afterwards, I'm in his arms. The last thing I want to do is leave. Bastien is a human furnace and the warmth he emanates makes me drowsily cheerful.

"Looks like we broke in the bed," I say into the perfection of his chest.

"We're just getting started, *kotyonok*."

An alarm goes off. Bastien stiffens. "Almost forgot," he grumbles. "We better get going."

"To what?"

"My brothers and mother land around midnight. We only have an hour or so."

"What?" I say, sitting up in alarm. "What are you talking about?"

"Get dressed," is all he says. Cryptic bastard.

"What am I getting dressed for?" I call out after him. But he's already disappearing down the hallway. I don't mind watching him go, if I'm being honest. I miss his warmth and his scent, but the sight of that man's muscular ass flexing with every step does dangerous things to me.

It occurs to me that all the hand-me-down sweats Bastien has been giving me to wear for the last few weeks are both A) in the basement and B) not suitable for any event whatsoever. I don't know what we're doing, but I know I can't wear that.

Acting on impulse, I get up and pad naked to a door I didn't notice before. When I open it, I see...

"Oh my God."

It's a walk-in closet, but I could probably charge four grand a month if I rented it out. The space is cavernous—and it's absolutely filled from top to bottom with clothes, shoes, purses.

"Holy... shit," I murmur to myself. I pace down the racks, my hands eagerly flipping through gorgeous dress after dress. "Holy—shit!"

I suddenly want to call up Kayla and video chat her all this. There's a laugh bubbling in me I'm not sure I should let out, lest it become an overwrought cry.

This is too amazing. Too wildly wonderful. Too good to be true.

It takes a few minutes for me to finally decide on a dress. I don't even bother trying to go through all of them—that would've taken almost an hour. Luckily, the only criteria I really had to abide by was "not too slutty." Apparently, I'm meeting Bastien's family, after all.

That seems a little sudden, seeing as how I was only just promoted from "basement prisoner" to "roommate," but the man only knows how to operate at one speed. Who am I to slow him down?

As I shower, put on makeup, and get dressed, I wonder idly what he's told them about me. *By the way, she was a stripper and worked for the Cubans.*

A shiver goes over me, although I shrug it off. Whatever Bastien told them, it probably wasn't that. He doesn't strike me as the type of guy to glom on the details.

I've just finished mascara-ing my upper lashes when Bastien comes to get me himself. "Didn't trust me to be ready in time myself?" I tease, picking up my purse.

"Not for a second," he says with a frank smile. "I'm no fool."

"You are many things, Bastien Nikolaev. But you are no fool."

He winks and hooks his arm in mine, and we're off.

The drive is quiet and uneventful. Although Bastien's hand clasp in the car is comforting, I can't seem to shake my nerves.

"Bastien…" I say.

"Don't worry," he says. "My family will love you."

"It's not just that," I say. "It's… José."

A new furrow appears on Bastien's forehead. "What about him?"

"I know you've probably got everything handled, I just… I know him. He loves symbolism. If he found out about this, then he'd do everything in his power to make sure it was you and your family's last supper."

"I've no doubt he's heard of it," Bastien says simply.

"But—"

"Melissa," Bastien sighs, "do you really think my Bratva would let an event like this go unguarded? We'll have snipers on nearby roofs, and men at every door. We've screened and double-screened anyone working or attending. Anyone who didn't pass muster has now found themselves out of a job. We have this handled. Trust me."

He puts his other hand on top of mine.

"I do trust you, you know." I lift my gaze to his with a little smile. "With my life."

"I know."

"Tell me more about your brothers," I say, to change the subject before I get too mushy-gushy. "Any pointers?"

"No pointers needed."

"How 'bout a pointer, singular?"

"Melissa," he chides, "there's nothing to worry about. They will like you. Trust me."

"You keep saying that. I'm starting to worry more."

"Fine. You want the Nikolaev dossier? Gavriil is the jokester of the family, the don of Boston. He's recently engaged to Hannah Hall, who will be here tonight as well. Dmitry is the oldest, the don of New York, and husband to Shannon. He's a father, too, as of not too long ago."

I nudge him with my elbow. "So Brothers 1 and 2 are engaged. Does that mean you just pulled me out of the basement since it was your turn?"

"Gavriil thought I should just bring a blow-up sex doll to dinner, but I told him you'd be more fun to drink with."

"Hey!" I give him a playful slap.

Bastien's gaze darkens. "Believe me, this was the last thing I wanted to happen."

"Oh, that's much better, thanks," I scoff. "My heart sings with joy."

He just shrugs. "You said you wanted the truth."

"I said that?"

"No, actually. But that's all I deal in. So you'll have to take it."

"So what happened?" I ask him, genuinely curious. "With us, I mean. You left looking like you wanted to kill me. And then you just... changed your mind?"

"You could say that."

"That's a little vague. Care to elaborate?"

Bastien eyes me with a gaze so piercing it makes me shift in my seat. Like he must be seeing my very soul, every bad and shitty thing I ever did.

"I saw you for what you are," he says quietly. "And that's all I needed to know."

"Oh." That's all I can say, after those words, under that gaze.

And then I settle my head on his shoulder, and I'm not worried anymore.

I'm just happy.

22

MELISSA

It's a happy daze, the next few minutes of quiet bliss.

And then, all too soon, we pull up to the restaurant. Bastien gets out first and holds the door for me. As soon as I'm out, his hand catches mine to help me to my feet.

We arrive through the restaurant's gilded two-story-high entranceway just as his brothers and mother pull up on the curb behind us.

"Bastien!" his mother exclaims, wrapping him in a hug accompanied by the click and clack of the many gold bangles on her wrists. "So good to finally see you."

A man who looks like a harsher version of Bastien chuckles as he leans over to say, "She hasn't shut up about how much she misses you. I think I'm demoted to third favorite son."

Bastien smirks and whispers back, "Hate to break it to you, but you've always been third, Gav."

Ah, so that must be Gavriil. And the other man shaking Bastien's hand now, the one with the same nose and cheekbones but narrower eyes—

that must be Dmitry.

"You should be proud," Dmitry tells Bastien. "Holding your own like you have here, with everything as disorganized and heated as it's been. But the Cubans will get what's coming to them soon enough."

Bastien inclines his head in agreement. "They will."

"Tonight will seal the deal," Gavriil agrees, throwing his arms around his brothers with a grin. "But first, let's eat, because I'm fuckin' *starving.*"

The two pretty women accompanying the Nikolaev brothers—one brunette, one blonde—hang back like I am while the boys talk. They see me looking and sweep over at once with big smiles.

"Hi!" says the blond brightly. "I'm Hannah."

"And I'm Shannon," adds the brunette.

"Melissa," I mumble to them. I wonder again what they've heard about me, what they think about me. Did I pick the right dress, the right shoes? Am I smiling too big, or not big enough?

But before I can stumble any more awkwardly through these introductions, Bastien strides over to wrap an arm around my shoulders. "Mother," he announces to the rail-thin woman with the piercing eyes, "this is Melissa."

She looks at me, cool and appraising. Is it because she always looks that way, or is there something about me in particular that needs a hard once-over?

"Hi," I say, extending a hand. *Stay cool, Mel. Everything is fine.* "It's nice to finally meet you."

"This is my mother," Bastien says to me. "Vanna."

I'm about to *nope* it the hell out of here, when Vanna's icy demeanor finally cracks. She extends a gracious hand and a smile. "Good to finally meet you as well, dear. I have been curious about the woman who has finally managed to steal my son's heart. I was starting to think he'd be a bachelor forever."

As elegant as she looks, her handshake is iron: strong and unforgiving.

"He is a good man," I tell her with a blush. "You did well."

"Yes," Vanna agrees. "I did, didn't I?"

"Business time," Bastien grunts. "Let's go, brothers. Ladies, we'll be back."

Without bothering to wait around for a response, he sweeps past the restaurant's gleaming tables, headed towards the back.

Vanna smirks wickedly. "While they have their fun, let's have ours."

Although, as we head to a private room in the back, passing Cubist portraits and Castilian guitar music from an odd-looking band, the word that comes to mind isn't "fun." Maybe for the three elegant women striding in first, but not for me.

More like "stressful-as-hell." That's three words, but you get the point.

I get that Bastien has a whole mysterious aura to cultivate at all times, but I'm a little irked that I didn't have more preparation on how to conduct myself here. Being left alone with three virtual strangers, one of whom is Bastien's own terrifying mother?

Not exactly a walk in the park.

"My dear," Vanna says, pausing.

My gaze shoots up, realizing it's me she's broken her light conversation with the others for. Even her kindest smile has a commanding air that makes me pity anyone who's had the misfortune to get on her bad side.

"You don't need to look so worried," she continues. "We don't bite."

"Us girls have to stay together," Shannon agrees with a nod.

Another confident, elegant, self-assured woman I already feel intimidated by?

Check, check, and... check.

"Sorry," I mumble. "This is still a lot to process."

"Don't apologize," Hannah says, shrugging a silk-sleeved shoulder. "The first time I met Vanna, my hands were sweating so much she asked if I forgot to dry them off."

"We also got shot at," Shannon chimes in with a rueful smile.

"Oh, did we? Forgot about that," Hannah chuckles sarcastically as she goes to sit down at the table. "You'll see, Melissa. Things can get pretty exciting around here."

"Not that exciting, I hope."

Everyone laughs appreciatively. Because it was funny or because they're pitying my discomfort? Probably a little helping of each, I'd imagine. But I'll take it. Little by little, I feel myself starting to unclench.

I can do this.

I follow them and pick an empty seat on the long table, across from Vanna, who's still looking at me with those dark eyes, liquid with blankness. A blankness that could mean just about anything.

What is it with this family and being unnecessarily cryptic?

"Bastien and I actually met during a little bit of chaos," I find myself blurting out. "So any more gunfights would be par for the course."

The two girls laugh, while Vanna straightens in her carved wooden seat with a sudden alertness, like a hawk spotting prey. "Bastien didn't mention how you met, actually."

"Oh." That might have been on purpose. Trust Bastien to be as tactful as I am tactless.

Vanna sighs with a wave of her hand, settling back in her seat, yet still somehow maintaining better posture than me. "Typical Bastien—*mum's the word,* always. Even as a baby, he'd hardly cry. He'd have the worst ear infection and I wouldn't know it for weeks. He'd just sit there, that chubby little meatball, with those big, beautiful eyes staring and staring, calm as could be." She redirects that gaze to me once again. "I'm sure you're much more talkative, right, Melissa? Tell us about you."

I gulp. *What should I tell them?*

That I'm a dancer? Former prisoner? A Cuban slave?

Or, probably more wisely, none of the above?

Finally, I force out an exhale. I can either sit here squirming and hope that things get better. Or I can be honest and upfront, and see what happens.

"I was a prisoner of the Cubans when Bastien met me," I tell them. "I was supposed to spy on him."

Three pairs of eyebrows fly up. My heart thumps.

"You can see how well that went," I tell them ruefully.

This silence has its own question: *How do we know you aren't spying now?*

"I don't know how to make you believe this," I say cautiously, "but I love Bastien with all my heart. I'd never do anything to hurt him."

More silence. I've never hated it more.

"My dear girl," Vanna says suddenly. "Look at me."

I look up into those intelligent silver eyes and swallow hard. It's easy to see where Bastien gets it from, that ability to pierce right through to the heart of me. His mom has been doing it since long before he was born.

"Of course you love him." She nods with approval. "I can see that. And Bastien is no fool. If he trusts you, I trust you."

A small smile is thinking of making its way onto my face, just maybe. "Thank you."

Vanna just chuckles. "Don't thank me. To be honest, it's your stir fry recipe that really won me over." She winks just to let me know she's teasing.

"Bastien told you that?" I ask.

She snorts. "It's about the only thing he would tell me. Nothing about your age or past, nothing. But I can see now myself that you're a strong woman, with a good head on your shoulders."

God, this feels like receiving a compliment from the Queen of England.

"And don't worry about how you met Bastien," Hannah chimes in. "I was Gavriil's employee, running his club."

"And I was part of an arranged marriage with an enemy mob," Shannon says. Seeing my face, she laughs and adds, "It's a long story."

That starts us off chatting easily, about each Nikolaev brother and their quirks. The wine that the waiter brings doesn't hurt. It seems only shortly after that that the boys return, all smiles and clapping Bastien on the back.

Gavriil waggles his brows as he slings himself beside Hannah. "What have you ladies been gossiping about?"

Shannon's smile is sweet. "Oh, just how lucky Bastien is to have found Melissa."

Bastien's scowl is half-amused. "Sounds about right."

As if on cue, the waiter swings by to refill our drinks and take our orders for food. He's barely a step away when Bastien tips his head to mine. "Everything okay?"

"I was super nervous," I admit in a low voice. "But everything's actually going great. Your mom, Shannon, and Hannah have been super nice."

Only someone who knows Bastien well could spot that a bit of tension just came out of his face. "Ah, good. I told her to take it easy on you. Not that I really expected her to."

"Thanks, I guess?"

He presses a kiss into my cheek. "No. Thank *you*."

"For?"

"Being here."

"It beats the basement."

The rest of the meal passes in a yummy, happy blur. Everyone is in happy, easy conversation with everyone else, the wine flows, the food is good. And with Bastien by my side, I don't feel nervous or afraid anymore... of anything.

It's a warm feeling. Safe. Like I don't have to be on my toes anymore, watching everything I do or say, watching everyone around me for signs of impending violence.

It feels like... crazily enough, I can actually do this.

I can see myself doing this—being here with all these wry, brazen Russians, by Bastien's side. I can see myself in this life in the future.

Maybe.

Bastien squeezes my hand and I come to. It takes me a few seconds to realize what's wrong: the music has stopped.

"It's your cue," Bastien leans over to whisper in my ear.

My forehead creases. "My cue... for what?"

Bastien rises and pulls me with him. "C'mon."

"Bastien," I say in an undertone, although I let him lead me to the adjoining room, "I don't think—"

"Don't worry," he says. "I'll be here."

Inside the main room, there's a raised platform I'd been too nervous to notice while coming through earlier. The raised platform has a microphone, is empty and unnoticed– for now.

Oh, God.

We pause in front of it.

"What's the matter?" he asks, eyeing me.

"It's just... I just..."

How to explain it? That, sure, I've loved singing all my life and this should just be another day, but it's not.

That a big part of me is overwhelmed by emotion already, and I'm not sure what would come out if I opened my mouth.

That today has already gone so well that I don't want to jinx it.

But Bastien's already leading me onto the stage. "You can do this."

Heads are turning our way. The band is clustered off to the side, watching us expectantly with instruments at the ready.

Bastien stalks up to the microphone and steps into his persona with an easy and carefree smile.

"And now, everyone—friends, family, colleagues, employees—I want to thank you for coming." We are lucky to have so many loved ones under one roof."

What a cute goof: hulking over the microphone, gripping it with two tense hands like it might run away. I'm smiling at first. Then I look out over the restaurant and realize with a heart-stopping lurch that *every single person in here is in the Bratva*. At least a hundred steely-eyed

Russians, expectant for whatever the hell Bastien is about to make me do.

"I have a special gift for you tonight," Bastien says. "Melissa?"

I swallow thickly. Funny, how I've sung into a microphone so many times I've lost track. Yet, this time, as I walk up to it and Bastien walks away to stand off the stage off to the side, I can feel my throat closing up as I do so.

It hits me all at once: *What song?*

Yeah, I could sing one of my usuals—a bunch of Spanish songs the Russians probably wouldn't care for. Probably not the best idea. As tight-lipped as Bastien has kept about me, word has to have gotten out.

And now, all these unfriendly, avid eyes rest on me.

I swallow, but the lump in my throat isn't going anywhere. Nor is the pounding in my head. *Think, Mel, think.* There has to be a song. There has to be something, some love song, something easy and inoffensive…

A smile flickers on my lips—that's it.

I force a cough—nope, looks like the throat lump is here to stay—then tell the band the name of the song.

They exchange a look. It's a weird choice, but my mind is pretty much blank at this point, so I'm gonna need them to just roll with it.

The drums start.

Then the guitar.

And then here I come, in three, two—

Oh shit, shit: what am I doing here?

I scan the crowd again and suddenly, my throat closes up. Ten years of conditioning has been drilled into me: *Trust no one.* But what I'm about to sing is trust of the highest order.

I can't sing this song to literal strangers, not with everything the lyrics confess. Maybe if Bastien and I were alone… but here?

My gaze lands on Bastien, off to the side. Not nervous in the slightest. Just expectant. Confident.

He believes in me.

So I can't let him down. Not after all he's done to make me feel safe.

Just in time to barely make my cue, I belt out: "Whenever I'm alone with you / You make me feel like I am home again / Whenever I'm alone with you / You make me feel like I am whole again…"

I'm not singing to the crowd, anyway. I'm singing to Bastien.

The man who saved my life in every way possible.

The one who showed me just what men are capable of, in the best way.

The more words and truth come out of me—"However far away, I will always love you"—the easier it gets. After all, I'm just telling him the truth. The words sing themselves out of me.

That final strum of the guitar fades out and shock blasts through me in its wake. The room is dead silent.

For half a second, I'm horrified. I've said too much. I've been obvious and naive.

But then, through the doorway, I see Vanna's teary face. Closer, Bastien is beaming.

I smile. The crowd erupts into applause.

You did it.

And at that exact moment, the far wall explodes.

23

BASTIEN

The air is sucked out of the room by the blast. Dust and the stench of gunsmoke replace it.

Someone is crying. Someone else is screaming.

Melissa—

I can't let anything happen to Melissa.

I charge to the stage. "Cover the hole!" I yell to my men.

They're already on their feet, racing from their tables. Behind me, I can hear Gavriil and Dmitry roaring instructions to their men, too. Ahead of me, Melissa is slowly climbing down off the stage, face dumbstruck.

I have to get there in time.

It's odd how, behind her, the band isn't reacting the way a gaggle of civilian musicians ought to do. They're moving with purpose and laser focus…

My hand leaps for my gun.

That's no band. Bands don't keep AK-47s in the drum kit.

"Get down, Melissa!" I bellow at her.

She wheels around, freezing at what she's seeing. What I should've seen—*Bastien, you fucking fool.*

It was the bassist, the one at the back of the stage. The one now taking off a greasy black wig and horn-wired glasses.

José fucking Correa.

It's already too late, but Melissa throws herself off stage the rest of the way. I race forward to catch her.

But I'm not close enough, not fast enough, and two of José's men who are closer leap forward and snatch her out of the air.

I do the only thing I can do: lift my gun and head-shot them both.

They topple off the stage, their suited bodies thumping on the wood floor. Melissa stumbles but manages to land on her hands and knees.

I'm almost there—so close…

But once again, not close enough.

Now, it's José grabbing her, arm hooking around her waist. He points a gun at her temple, although his ugly smile is aimed right at me.

"Come a little closer, Russian. Go on, try it."

The killing gleam in his eyes urges me: *I dare you.*

I skid to a stop a few feet away. Behind me, there's shooting and shouts from our side, Cuban voices raised in gleeful bloodlust as they pour through the hole from the recent explosion on the opposite side. Twenty, fifty, a hundred of them, I can't even tell.

We're down dozens of men already. The debris took out five or six tables full of Bratva men seated near the wall, and the first wave of gunfire through the smoke cleared another handful. It's a fucking travesty.

I switch my gaze back to José. I'm surprised he hasn't made a move yet.

Instead, he's scowling, his expectant glance over his shoulder as he mutters something in Spanish. Maybe another bomb failed to go off.

Whatever it is, I can't focus on that. Can't focus on any but the way this son of a bitch is gripping Melissa—like she's some piece of meat. Like she belongs to him.

I want to bury a bullet in his skull so bad it itches. But I can't risk Melissa. There has to be another way.

"Another screw-up?" I ask him, gesturing to where he was looking. The longer I can keep him distracted, the better.

José's colorless eyes flicker to me angrily, and I know I'm right.

"This was a surprise," I growl, keeping my sight locked on him. "You got that much right, at least."

José's smile is eerily mild. "We got a lot more than that right."

His gaze flickers behind me at the unfolding scene. I take another quick glance that way, too, still struggling to make sense of what I'm seeing. As much sense you can make of pure chaos.

The charging Cubans don't even seem to be aiming where they're spraying their bullets.

That matches the reports I've heard: that they aren't too picky about who they kill. Young or old, man or woman, mobster or innocent bystander—it doesn't matter to them; death is death. By the looks of it, they're even hitting some of their own frontrunners.

Vicious fuckers just want blood.

Of the Bratva men who survived the initial onslaught, damn near every single one of them has reacted the way they ought to. They've shoved tables on their sides into makeshift barriers and started returning fire. For right now, at least, the flow of Cuban assholes through the gap in the wall has slowed. But the room is bright and loud with gunfire.

"It takes a whole lot more to win a war," I tell José.

My gaze goes to Melissa—*I will get you out of this.*

"I'll be fine," she cries out. "Just go!"

"Not a fucking chance."

"You should listen to the girl." José's voice is pleasant as he walks them backwards on the stage without ever moving the gun from her temple. "She may not be smart, but she's right about this."

"Shut your mouth," I growl at him. "I don't want to hear a word you have to say."

I inch forward at the same slow rate that he's inching backward.

At the crash of nearby movement, I whirl around and shoot a Cuban in the neck just as he raises his gun to shoot me.

"Suit yourself." Now, José is tracing a tender circle on Melissa's cheek with the nozzle of the gun. "You'll only get yourself killed. She'll get to watch."

"You are delusional, Correa." A bullet buries itself at my feet. I turn and shoot where it came from. I don't even wait to see the shooter's body hit the floor. "You and your men are finished."

Keeping my attention divided between José and the Cubans who think I'm a distracted target isn't easy, but it's necessary. I won't leave Melissa to be taken by him. No fucking way.

"Finished playing games with you boys, yes. Finished altogether? You are quite wrong about that, my friend."

Then he backs into the swinging kitchen door as Melissa screams.

I burst through after them. Running into an unscoped room is as stupid as it gets, but fuck the rules and procedures; this is my woman he's pawing. I'll do whatever it takes to get her back.

I dive behind a prep table as soon as I enter the kitchen. But when I stand up, all I see is more cooking equipment. Some still smokes; some still sizzles. There isn't a person in sight.

Fuck.

Then, at the far end of the room, I see a door swinging subtly. *That way.*

I sprint to it, kick it open, and catch José trying to drag Melissa around the corner. It looks like she's clamped her teeth down on his forearm. He's bleeding and swearing and as I watch, he clips her hard in the jaw with the gun. Her bite slackens. Her scream makes my blood curdle.

"Let her go!" I roar. "Let her go and I might even kill you mercifully."

José just smiles, transferring the nozzle of his gun back to Melissa's temple. "I like my odds as they are."

Seeing Melissa like this—fists gripped on her own dress impotently, green eyes wide and flat with shock—makes my clutch tighten on the gun.

It hurts how much I'm tensing the finger to keep it from instinctively going for the trigger.

No matter the odds, I've never held back a shot like this. Never. I've always been the best shot, the fastest. But I can't bet on that this time. I can't take that risk.

Rush this—and I could kill her.

No, I need to time it right. I won't get a second chance.

I pause and, keeping half my focus on José, I use the other half to get a sense of my bearings.

The back half of the kitchen is much the same as the first. Gleaming chrome appliances, pots left boiling over when everybody fled at the sound of the explosion. I see vegetables left half-diced, knives still stuck in the cutting boards.

"I was so hurt when I learned what you'd done," José says to Melissa. Really, though, he's talking to me. Taunting me with her vulnerability. Daring me to do something about it.

He continues, "After all those years we took care of you, fed you, clothed you, gave you a place to stay. We treated you like family—and this is how you repay us? By taking up with dirty fucking Russians? By *betraying* us?"

When she still doesn't answer, he shakes her again.

"Take your hands off her," I growl.

José's gaze slinks to me, almost bored, as though remembering I'm here. All part of his act. Sick men like him live for these dog-and-pony shows. "You misunderstand. 'On her' is where my hands belong. She is mine, after all."

"Wrong again."

José bares a smile of long teeth. "I raised the bitch. Or didn't she tell you?" He sighs mournfully. "No matter. Now, it's time for her to come home."

"I will kill you," I snarl. "I will cut you down like a fucking sheep."

"Oh, I don't doubt you'd *like* to." His voice is pleasant, his gaze coy. "Many men have wished the same thing. And yet here I stand."

If I didn't know better, I'd think this man was a coward, a weasel. He's at least a foot and a half shorter than me and a hundred pounds lighter. Pudgy and skinny at the same time, slack-jawed, dull-eyed.

The face of a man who was meant to glide through history unnoticed and die without so much as a single person attending his funeral.

But he chose a different path for himself.

He made himself into a kingpin. He made himself into the god of Miami.

And now, he's made himself into a dead man walking.

I need to tread carefully, though. One look at José and I can see it: people have been underestimating him his entire life. It would be easy to make the same mistake—too easy.

And fatal for one or both of us.

"You did this to yourself, you know," José remarks. "You came to my city, so arrogant and proud, and thought you could simply take, take, take. Typical Russians—you only care about yourselves. Not about what is the best for your people, your city. I could have let you go quietly—if you had agreed to leave."

"Somehow, I don't believe that," I drawl.

He chuckles. "Perhaps not. The best parting gift for a Russian is a knife in the back, I've learned. I've brought you just such a present. Would you like it now?"

"Come and give it to me," I taunt him, dropping low into a fighting stance. "If you can."

He just clicks his teeth like he's disappointed. "You are a brutal man, Bastien Nikolaev—but so *direct*. Don't you know that you don't always have to take the hardest path forward? Every man has his weaknesses. Much, much easier to go for those."

He strokes Melissa's fallen hair from her cheek and presses a soft kiss there. Even from across the room, I can see her shudder.

"I was hoping to get Gavriil and Dmitry's women," he continues. "But since you have a hard-on for this whore, she'll have to do."

Just then, a flash of movement as Melissa's hand jabs down to grab—
to grab what?

Ultimately, it doesn't matter. José smacks her over the head with the
gun and she crumbles down with a pained cry.

A roar slips out of my mouth as I lift my gun to shoot. But José is
already raising his and firing.

In the next second, pain explodes into my left shoulder where it meets
my neck. Half an inch closer to the midline and I'd be dead.

I fire back with my good arm. Bullets ricochet everywhere. My shots
slow him, but don't stop him: there's too many fucking appliances and
counters and bullshit in the way.

Until he pops out into the line of fire. and I can get him, if I just aim
carefully, right *there*, so I pull the trigger and—

CLICK. Empty. No more bullets.

I snarl and hurl my gun to the side. I'm diving for cover, but I'm too
slow. José is grinning as he stands up and aims the kill shot.

I'm a sitting duck with no way to defend myself.

This is it.

But instead of the final crack of a bullet, I hear that noise one more
time.

CLICK.

He's out, too. I hear him swearing in Spanish instead, then the crash of
a gun being tossed to the side.

Our glares meet in understanding.

Time to solve this the old-fashioned way.

Next second, we're racing for each other. The pain from my shoulder is pounding through my body, but I leap onto him with a guttural roar.

Our hands grip each other as we wrestle. Little fucker is wiry, strong. My injured arm being a useless piece of shit doesn't help, either. Hot sweat and blood coats us both. My vision starts to blur.

Seeing his advantage, José presses his fingers into the open wound on my shoulder. I bellow in pain.

With his other hand, he brandishes a knife—*when the fuck did he pick that up?*—and tries to bring it down on my exposed throat.

I raise my hand just in time to stop the descent. My fingers clamp around his, but they're slick with blood, so I can't wrench the blade out of his grasp.

We're both struggling, flexing, slipping and sliding on the kitchen floor helplessly, with death hanging in the balance.

Then, to my horror, my hand slips. There's just too much blood to hold on tight. José's eyes are bright with bloodlust and the knife is coming, coming, coming—

And then it stops and falls clattering from José's suddenly limp hand.

José shudders. My gaze snaps to Melissa, standing tall over his shoulder.

Then to José's neck.

And there, I see a glint of brass shining amongst an ocean of blood.

It's my house key.

I want to say something to her. Tell her that I love her, that I need her, that I'll take on the whole world if it means keeping her safe.

But the fight is over and with it goes my adrenaline. Which was apparently the only thing keeping me conscious.

My vision fades. José slumps heavy and dead on top of me. And above it all is her.

Whatever happens to me, the most important thing is that she's safe now. She's free.

Melissa is going to be alright.

24

MELISSA

It's funny—whenever Kayla and I used to watch horror movies and the main character would do something unrealistically stupid or pathetic, like freeze up as the monster was about to rip out their throat, I would always swear up and down that, if faced with the same situation, I would be no better. I would freeze up. Freak out. Be utterly and completely useless.

And yet as soon as I see Bastien slump to the floor, I'm racing by his side.

Even as I cradle his head in my lap, his eyes are fluttering shut. "Don't you dare, Bastien Nikolaev," I admonish him. "Don't you dare pass out on me."

I look around frantically. José is slumped off to Bastien's side, dead as a doornail. Good riddance to that evil bastard.

But that's not what's important right now. Beyond him, hot pasta water is surging over the sides of the pot onto the floor. I follow the trickle down, past spent bullet cartridges and blood running through the grooves in the tile to see—*yes*, a towel.

I grab it and press it to Bastien's shoulder. It's instantly soaked through. Blood, so much blood...

I rip my gaze away and force my breathing to remain calm. If I freak out, Bastien dies. Simple as that. I have to keep a clear head, figure out what to do.

He's not going to last long like this. He needs help—and the closest help is outside that door to the restaurant, where I can still hear shooting and the odd strangled cry.

The fight is still raging fiercely. Trying to fetch help might just lead some Cubans straight here or get me shot myself. I won't do Bastien much good if I'm dead.

My gaze slips to the back door. It isn't super far. Maybe if I just—

I grab his uninjured shoulder and start to pull. It does precisely... nothing.

"Goddammit," I mutter. The man is *heavy*.

I grab his arm again and pull with everything I have. He shifts half an inch.

Yeah, sure, I can move him. It just might take the rest of my natural life to get him to that back door. He won't last that long in this state.

"Dammit, dammit, dammit!" I swear, slamming my palm into the tile repeatedly.

I sink to a seat at Bastien's side and glance back and forth between the two doors. One leads away from danger. One leads into it. Both seem impossible.

But I have to choose.

So I use the counter to pull myself to my feet, take a deep breath—and charge to the door that leads back into the restaurant.

I open the door a crack and peer out. From what I can see, the room is split, with each side holding one half. Based on the large number of Cuban corpses on the floor, it looks like the Russians are winning.

That doesn't mean it's safe, though. All it takes is one stray shot to find me—and there's plenty to spare out there.

"Let's go," I mutter to myself. Then, before I can second-guess myself, I make a break for it.

I sprint across the room, bullets crashing into where I was seconds before. It's chaos in here. Pure fucking chaos.

But as I run, I almost understand why Bastien likes this sort of thing. Talk about an adrenaline rush. I've never felt more alive.

"Get out of there!" I hear Vanna yell from the bar she and Shannon are hiding behind.

She's right: out in the open like this, I'm a sitting duck. A running duck, rather. Target practice for the Cuban army.

But I can't go back now. Not until I've found help.

The nearest Bratva man is Dmitry, crouching behind a table and shooting intermittently. I race to him, and all my words come out in a hurried jumble. "It's Bastien—he's been shot—bad—kitchen—blood loss, he passed out. Needs help. He needs help!"

"Lead the way," he says grimly, as calm as could be.

We pick the safest path possible back to the kitchen as the Bratva soldiers provide cover fire. I'm hopeful. *It's all gonna be okay.*

Until I step inside and my heart sinks.

He's where I left him, surrounded by even more blood. His skin looks too pale and it's clammy to the touch.

"Please, God, no," I whimper.

More Bratva men pour in after us. They work fast, quickly hefting him up and away towards the back door that seemed so far when I was trying to drag him myself.

As they carry him out, I stride by his side, holding his hand. "It's going to be alright, I promise," I whisper to him. "It has to be."

It has to be.

The next week passes in a blur.

Over-salted hospital fast food. The smell of industrial-strength disinfectant. His brothers and their wives, his mother, an endless succession of stone-faced doctors.

One nurse is nice; the other is bitchy. The fluorescent lights are too bright and their droning gives me a headache.

I sleep on a cot they leave in the room for me. I sing to Bastien when it's just us. I think he'd like that.

Today, I'm singing that same song from what seems so long ago. *"Whenever I'm alone with you / You make me feel like I am home again / Whenever I'm alone with you / You make me feel like I am whole again..."*

The last notes fade away. My eyes are closed—mostly to keep the tears at bay, at least for a little while—which is why I hear him before I see him.

"Keep... going..."

I wrench my eyes open to see Bastien looking back at me. He's smiling —or trying to, at least, though it looks more like a grimace of pain.

He clutches my hand weakly. Then his grip slackens and his eyes flutter closed again.

I curl up at his side and wait. He'll make it. I know he will.

Not everyone I love will die.

The next day, I have a visitor.

It's Dmitry who brings her in. "Oh my God, Kayla!" I exclaim as soon as I see that first flash of bright purple nails.

I race for her and tackle her in a hug. If it weren't for the wall, we would've hit the floor in a tangle of limbs.

I squeeze the life out of her, and then plant a sloppy kiss on her cheek for good measure. When I pull away, she's smiling from ear to ear.

"Babe, babe, it's so good to see you."

She smells the same: that warm, peachy perfume she used whenever José wasn't insisting we coat ourselves in eau de guava.

I take a step back and search her pale, freckled face. "You… Does this mean…?"

Kayla just nods, her auburn ponytail bobbing, with a smile so big and broad that it makes me beam right back.

"Just like that," I murmur. I can't quite believe it.

"Just like that," she echoes with a wry grin. "After word of José's death got out, the infighting started. He was what was holding the Cubans together—they were all scared shitless of him."

"What'd you do?"

"Me?" She shrugs. "It wasn't too hard to slip away when José's usual guard dogs were out there vying for power and choosing sides like the rest of them." She tilts her head to the side and looks at me with an amused sparkle in her eye. "What about you? If half of what I heard is true—"

"Oh God, do I even want to know?"

Kayla's already chuckling. "Well, the story goes that you single-handedly fought off José and kicked his sorry ass into the afterlife. That you led him into a trap that snapped the Russians shut on him and his men. That you've been working for the Bratva from the start."

I chuckle, too. The reality is both wilder and way tamer than the story. "And what do *you* think?" I tease.

Kayla slings herself in a seat, her blue daisy-print dress settling all around her in a final puff of peach scent. "I think you're going to tell me."

And so I do. I tell her it from the very start: from meeting Bastien and being locked up in the basement, to how, bit by bit, we fell for each other. To the night at the restaurant when I thought everything was over.

"So you did stab José," Kayla says when I'm done. "I always knew you were a bad bitch."

"It wasn't that impressive." I reach over to squeeze Bastien's unconscious hand. "Bastien was the one who got the job done."

Kayla looks unconvinced. "But still—a key to the throat? That's badass. They should make a movie about you." Her voice drops into a more somber tone. She fixes me with a serious look and says, "Did it feel good? He had it coming. He deserved worse, actually. You kinda let him off easy."

"Honestly? It felt amazing." I'm mindlessly massaging Bastien's hand like a stress ball. "We spent so long living with his leash around our throats, Kay. So many years cowering in his shadow. Even when I was locked up in Bastien's basement, I felt safer than anywhere else—and yet, in the back of my mind, José was still there. Waiting. He really did a number on me."

Kayla nods emphatically. "Preach, sister. When I heard he was dead, I felt like a chain around my neck finally got cut off. I couldn't understand why everyone I met on the street or out and about wasn't grinning their faces off like I was. And now that I'm free..."

Her gaze meets mine, then shies away. She knows. Of course she knows.

Free. A word so innocuous, so easily taken for granted. And yet a word that was out of reach for us for so, so long.

Now that we have it, it feels too good to be true. Free to make our own choices, be our own people? Free to lock our own doors at night? It can't be.

But it is.

"He *is* handsome." Kayla's peering at Bastien's sleeping face. "Though I guess we'll have to do introductions later."

"He'll love you," I promise.

Kayla quirks a brow. "Oh?"

I slap her playfully. "Not like *that*, you ho."

She grins. "Just messin' with ya, you smitten kitten."

I blush, but another wave of relief settles over me. That was something else I'd worried about: how things between Kayla and I might be after all this.

But now, it's clear that there was no reason to worry. Kayla and I lived through hell together. Not a damn thing in the world can tear us apart now.

Kayla bites her lip. "Actually, I have something to tell you, too. Someone you'll have to meet."

"No way." I lock eyes with her, to see if she's screwing with me. "Not Pierre?"

Kayla nods, cheeks aflame. "The one and only."

"But how…?"

"Simple. I walked right up to him and kissed him yesterday." Over my laughter, she adds, "Our second date is tonight."

"I would wish you good luck," I tell her with a nudge, still laughing. "But you two are soulmates, so…"

Kayla just grins.

That's another thing we're free to do: love. José scared away anyone who dared get near us for so, so long that I almost forgot it's possible to feel the love of a man and not be fearful for his life. By the look in her eyes, Kayla knows exactly what I'm talking about.

She can venture out into that world now. Maybe she'll get her heart broken, maybe she'll get married and have thirty kids. But she'll be free to choose her own path. You can't put a price on that.

"Anyway," Kayla says, checking her phone, "I have to get ready for that, so I should go. But let's go shopping later this week?"

"Definitely down," I tell her. "I'm sorry I haven't—"

"Don't apologize," she cuts me off. "Bastien was hurt; I get it. You've been through a lot lately too. Anyway, I hope he gets better soon."

We part with a hug.

"Oh, almost forgot," she says, lingering at the door. "Some more good news. Thanks to the infighting amongst the Cubans, it sounds like the Russians have pretty much taken over Miami." She flicks her chin at Bastien. "Looks like you might've just hooked up with a king."

And then she's gone, leaving me thinking.

I suppose it doesn't really matter at the end of the day. New don of Miami or not, Bastien will always be *my* king.

~

The next few days are a slow unrolling. Bastien grumbles at his bandages and what he calls the "mealworm" food the hospital provides.

"Jesus, I know you hate the food," I grumble when he squeezes my thigh between reluctant bites of what the cafeteria is generously calling Swedish meatballs. "I'll go get you something better. No need to get handsy."

"That's not it," he says quietly.

"Then what is?"

"I wanted to wait for us to be alone," he says, hand gliding up and down my forearm. "Thought it was obvious."

I snort. "With you, nothing is obvious."

"After this, things will be different."

"Yeah?" My grumbly expression breaks with the start of a smile that wants to believe, but doesn't. Not quite. Not yet.

"Yeah. Equals. Not captor and prisoner."

"Gee, how generous."

Bastien winces playfully. "Guess I deserve that."

"You deserve a whole lot more than that, buster."

I laugh, but he doesn't. He's got that serious Bastien look in his eyes. Like he's waiting for something.

"Well?" he finally says.

"Well." I eye him. The beautiful swoop of that nose. The proud cliff of his chin. "That's a relief. Since I wasn't looking forward to escaping from here. Are you sure, though?"

"You're joking."

"Just... before... you seemed so—"

"Of course I'm sure," he says. "I know what I want, and it's you, Melissa. Besides—you saved my life."

"No." I twist mine around to thread my fingers between his into my own squeeze. "You saved mine."

With a sudden jolt, he pulls me to him, my lips falling onto his.

"Bastien!" I scold, pulling away. "The doctor said—"

With effort, he reaches up to cup the back of my head and pull me back to him. "Fuck the doctor. Come here."

And over the next few minutes, Bastien shows that he's quite a bit more healed than any of us thought.

By the time his family is back with the outside food he demanded, Bastien's out cold and snoring. We settle down to eat in the chairs around his bed. But one look at the garlic mashed potatoes sends me rushing to the bathroom to puke my guts up.

"What the hell?" I moan at my vomit in the toilet.

I don't get sick. Not ever. Not even from those awful fish tacos at El Palacio that gave half the girls food poisoning for a week.

But come to think of it, my body *has* been acting off lately.

Like my period, for instance. When was the last time...

I flush the toilet, turning away with a lurch. No way. No goddamn way.

Good thing I'm in a hospital. Pregnancy tests are not exactly in short supply.

I buy one from the downstairs pharmacy, lock myself in a stall, pee on it, and wait. Breathing hard, heart pounding.

When two blue lines appear, I stare at them like I can erase the second one if I try hard enough.

Oh, God.

Will this ruin everything?

25

BASTIEN

Sunset slants in through the back bay windows, casting the wrought-iron patio table into a reflective gold. The garden is a playground of shadow and light. An early evening breeze flutters past us like a kiss.

Melissa's back is to me as she continues setting the table, but I don't need to see her smile to know that it's devilish as she speaks.

"… We'll tell them you saved my life from a vicious mugging at the hands of a notorious criminal and got shot in the process."

"That could work." I wrap my arms around her. "But let's go with 'kidnapping attempt.' Makes me sound more heroic."

She lets out a little sigh, one of those many soft noises she makes that I love so much. "Bastien."

"Melissa."

She lets her head loll into my chest, although she keeps the rest of her body tense. "Keep touching me like that and we're never going to be ready for them."

I tighten my hold around her, dipping my face into her hair. I know she hates it, but I can't get enough of that guava scent. "And that'd be a bad thing because…?"

Digging an elbow into my gut, Melissa slips away and a wagging, scolding finger. "I'm not going to dignify that with a response."

I sigh mournfully as she resumes setting the table. "Fine. Back to the story."

She bites her lip, scrutinizing her fork placement and adjusting it slightly. "Maybe kidnapping attempt wouldn't be the worst idea. You know, sticking to the truth as much as possible is the cardinal rule of lying." She puts a hand on her hip and gives her head a regal tilt. "You could add on that I'm European royalty, to add a bit of flair. A princess from Transnistria or somewhere like that."

"Trans-what?"

"It's a country, you bozo. At least, I think it is. Or—wait." Her eyes flare with mirth as she brainstorms. "Maybe you went to boot camp to re-enlist, but it kicked your ass so hard that you're rethinking it?"

"Great." I put a glass down on the table with a hard clack. "So instead of looking like a hero, I look like a bitch."

"You look like a soldier," she corrects. "It's believable."

"True," I agree. "Although, as I said, we could always just call this off and reschedule at a later date. One when we have our stories straight. If we wait long enough, I might even be all healed up, and we wouldn't even need a story."

Melissa pauses and directs a sidelong frown my way. "You really want to do that?"

I shake my head. "No. God knows Randy will be pestering me every other day again if I do. Better to just get it over with. Like ripping off a Band-Aid."

"Yeah," Melissa agrees quietly.

I eye her. Ever since I got out of the hospital a few days back, she's been quiet, withdrawn. Her bursts of sassing and humor are fewer and farther between.

My hand catches hers before she walks away. I tug her to me, but even now, she doesn't quite want to meet my eye.

"What?" she asks, a little flustered.

I hold firm. "I could ask you the same thing."

Melissa extricates herself. "Now is not the time to be cryptic, Bastien. What is it?"

"Something's wrong with you." I hold her in place so I can scrutinize her. "And I don't know what it is."

"What makes you say that?" Melissa won't meet my eye, but then again, she's always claiming my eyes are "too intense for normal conversation," so maybe I'm just being paranoid.

But I know her. I don't think I am.

"Don't sidestep the question."

She sighs. "It's probably nothing. It's just…" She bites at the inside of her lip, then exhales out her nostrils. "I was theirs for so long that I can't believe it's really over. That José won't just show up out of nowhere and drag me back."

I wrap my arms around her, enjoying the softness of her body against mine. This is where she belongs—in my embrace. "That's not going to happen."

"I know." She squirms, without success, to disengage herself, then finally sighs, letting herself enjoy it at last. "I told you it was nothing."

"We've taken over all the Cubans' businesses," I continue. "Executed the few who dared trying to resist and exiled the rest. The Cubans are finished, princess. You'll never have to worry about them again."

She smiles sadly. "Keep talking. I like it when you say things like that."

My hands go to her shoulders, start massaging out the tension there. "I'm the don of Miami now. This is our home. I'm going to keep you safe here."

She relaxes herself into my arms, and from above, I can't tell what her face looks like. If my words worked or not.

But something in my gut says not quite all the way. It's just a feeling, and I don't normally take much stock of those.

Just feels like there's something she isn't telling me.

I don't get a chance to keep delving, though, because just then, there's a knock at the door. I answer to see Randy and Amy standing on the doorstep, arms full of lunch goods, with matching huge smiles on their faces.

"Oh, isn't this nice!" Amy gushes as I lead them to the back. She gestures to the back garden beyond the patio. "I don't think I've ever seen so many lilacs in one place."

"They were my mother's favorite," Melissa says as she pours drinks for everyone. "And Bastien gave me free rein with the garden, so—Lilac Central it is."

"Better you than me," I say with a chuckle. "It'd be a field of dirt if I was in charge."

Randy laughs. "I'm with you there, neighbor. Let me tell you: Amy is a whiz with the flowers. Me? The blackest of thumbs."

Amy pats him gently on the shoulder. "As I've told you, darling, if you water them all day every day, you drown the poor little things."

"Well, so be it. I know where I do and don't belong." Randy's pudgy face is pink but pleased as he turns his gaze to me. "At any rate, I'm glad we could finally do this, Bastien."

"We are, too," I say. "And again, we can't apologize enough for 'Golfballgate.'"

Randy holds up a hand. "Don't. I learned an important lesson that day, one I should've known already—stay the hell out of other people's houses. And I'm restricting all practice to the driving range now, too."

"Besides…" Amy is already casting a sympathetic blue eye over at me, my arm in a sling. "We couldn't stay mad even if we wanted to. Just look at the state of you!" She adds in a low voice, "I think it's so brave that you tried to enlist again, even if it… didn't end up well."

I wince.

I'm not particularly pleased that Melissa went with the 'boot camp kicked his ass' explanation mere seconds after the Finches walked through the door, but she thinks it's hilarious and it's easier than explaining the truth.

No way would the real story go down well. *I'm fine, neighbor—it was only a shootout between us and the Cuban mafia, no need to worry. They won't be bothering us for a long time now. I'm part of the Russian Bratva after all. In fact, I run the whole damn thing.*

They'd run screaming for the hills, and honestly, I don't want that. I'm starting to like this neighborhood, sheepdog and all. I might even stay.

"Those cookies you sent yesterday helped," Randy says. "After half a dozen of those, I couldn't have stayed upset with you if I tried."

"All Melissa," I defer.

"It was my pleasure," she says. "Getting this one to eat is a struggle and a half, so I'm happy to have someone who'll enjoy what I bake."

"If I ate all *this* one made me," I shoot back, "I wouldn't fit in the house."

We all chuckle at that. I steal another quick squeeze of Melissa's hand under the table, and it hits me all at once: this time with the Finches feels different. It's not just for show, these smiles, these jokes, these laughs—it's real.

I'm actually enjoying this, God knows how.

As I limp to the bathroom, I cast a look back. Randy and Amy are telling a story, Melissa grinning as she tilts back her juice cup to take a sip.

She looks beautiful, of course. *Really settled into domestic bliss, haven't you?* an ironic voice snarls in my head.

I shift my shoulders uneasily. It's right.

Hell, I thought Dmitry and Gavriil were insane when they threw themselves into this kind of life. Yet, I have to admit, it does have its upsides.

Or, in my case, one upside in particular.

It's been weird waking up warm and smiling next to her since we got home from the hospital. I haven't even touched a gun in over a week, but I don't have that familiar itch to check and recheck the ammo. To make sure I'm ready for war at the drop of a hat.

The urge is just… gone.

Returning to the table, I find Melissa leaning over, looking at Amy's phone.

"… I dug these old baby photos out of storage the other day, and now, I can't stop looking at them," Amy enthuses. "Would you look at those chubby cheeks? God, Helen was a cutie."

"No kidding." Melissa's face is beaming, but odd, wearing a look I can't place. "She was absolutely adorable."

"You'll see," Randy says confidently. "You can think babies are cute right now, but when you have your own: *bam!* Whole new world."

"I'll bet," Melissa says quietly.

Our gazes meet. Long enough to catch a slight sheen on hers. She looks away.

Fuck, am I imagining things?

Later that night, once Amy and Randy have left, I make my move. Melissa tries to make all sorts of excuses: that she has to call Kayla, clean up, take out the garbage.

But finally, I corner her.

"Melissa," I say.

"Really, Bastien, I—"

"Don't," I growl. "Tell me."

"Tell you what?" Her voice has all the cluelessness of the innocent, except she won't meet my eye.

"Whatever it is that's really bothering you. What's going on."

"I told you." She makes to move past me. "It's nothing."

I block her. "I'm not letting you go until you tell me."

Fire flashes in her eyes as they leap to me. "Oh, it's back to this, is it? You're in charge and I have no choice but to listen to you?"

"Melissa." I grit my teeth to stay calm. "Please."

She exhales, looking away again. "Do we have to do this now? I had such a good time and…"

"And whatever you have to say would ruin that? Melissa, just tell me what's happening with you."

Her gaze sneaks to mine, then falls again. "I was just thinking… if you're against getting too close to me, then how would we handle a baby?"

I blink in surprise. Out of all the things I expected Melissa to confess, this wasn't one of them.

"When did I ever say that?" I ask. "That I was against getting too close to you?"

"Actions speak louder than words," she says quietly. "I see it in your eyes, your hands. You're afraid of this."

"Listen to me," I snarl, stepping close to her. "I'm not afraid of a goddamn thing. I've seen everything there is to be afraid of in this world. But when I look at you, there's no fear. Not a drop of it. When I look at you, all I see is what could be."

She's quiet. Her eyes are misty with unshed tears.

"As for a baby," I continue, "where is this coming from?"

She says nothing.

"Melissa. Are you pregnant?"

"What if I am?" she whispers. She's bracing already for the answer she fears.

It hits me like a tidal wave. She's pregnant. With my baby.

"It's okay," she says with a sort of stiltedness that seems way too prepared for this. Like a line for a play she practiced in the mirror again and again. "I know this is all way too fast, that we were just starting to get used to each other. I'll understand if this is too much right now, but of course you're welcome in the baby's life, even if you don't want much to do with me—"

I catch her by the hand. "What the hell are you talking about?"

"You don't have to do this," she says quietly, eyes tilted with proud sadness. "I don't want your pity."

I let her hand drop. "When did I ever say anything about pity?"

"I know you, Bastien." She turns away. "You hardly wanted to let me into your life, and now this? It's too much. I get it."

"Don't speak for me."

Her gaze snaps back to me, hopeful and fearful at the same time.

"This has been one crazy roller coaster ride," I say. "That doesn't mean I don't know what I want. I've told you before: I always know what I want."

"Bastien, you're not saying…"

"I want you, Melissa." I grasp her hand and hold it tight. "I want our baby."

I lean in and kiss her on the cheek. Her body presses against mine, then draws away a fraction, eyes closing with a head-to-toe sigh.

But she can't quite unclench all the way just yet. She's waiting.

For me to say more—or take it all back.

"Enough of this bullshit." I bring her hand to my lips and press a kiss onto her knuckles. "We'll be a family. The three of us."

Her hand is trembling in mine as her gaze searches my face. "You mean it?"

"Let me show you how much."

My lips go to hers, my hands to her belly. "I want you," I whisper. "And I want this baby."

Melissa sighs into my mouth. "Say that again."

"I want you. I want this baby. I want you. I want this baby. I want all of it, everything you have. And everything I have is yours."

She kisses me back harder, her body giving into mine as my massaging hands drag over her, in rediscovery, enjoyment, hope.

She feels so damn good in my arms. So right.

I kiss her into the TV room and onto the long leather couch. I kiss off the green polka dot summer dress that brings out her eyes until she's nearly naked before me.

On top of her, I drink in the beautiful, tan curves of her body, even as she squirms under my gaze.

"What are you doing?" she asks.

"Enjoying you," I say. Then I cover her mouth with mine.

She smells like guava and tastes like everything I've ever wanted.

Fucking hell do I love her.

I love how her body fits with mine. I love how she moves with me. I love how she brings me out of myself.

I love every damn thing about her.

Every kiss is more heated than the last. Her tongue answers mine. Her pelvis is arcing up to meet me before I've even got her panties off.

They're wet with excitement; I'm hard with it. Her legs are hooked around me, holding me close, pulling me closer.

Goddamn.

Already, Melissa has been so many things to me. Enemy. Prisoner. Lover. Girlfriend. Partner.

Now, mother of my child? It's too much to believe.

She rips off my shirt and I pull off her bra. Her breasts bounce with our grinding hips. I cup one in each hand, nip at her neck, breathe my lust right into her skin.

"Fucking gorgeous," I growl.

"Bastien," is all she can manage to say. "Give it to me."

I like that desperate look, but I'm greedy. I want to see more of it. "Say please."

"Ass!" she hisses. She pulls out of the kiss, taking my lip partway.

I squeeze her breasts hard and she groans and crumbles forward, forehead coming to rest against my chest.

"You..." she says, breathing heard, pussy pressed right up against my erection. "You..."

"I love you," I say. "That's what."

All the fight, even joking, goes out of us. Our lips find each other again. We strip the last of these useless clothes away and melt into each other.

She's so soft, so good, so mine. And with every grind of our hips together, every drop of sweat and heavy sigh we share, she becomes more mine. I become more hers.

I flip her to her knees and take her from behind. I put her on her back and drive so deep into her I wonder if she can take it all.

But of course she can. Melissa is made of tough stuff.

"You're mine, Melissa." I pull her to me and thrust my cock further into her. "And I'm yours."

And when I thrust into her again, I can feel the walls of her pussy contract and tighten as her body sinks onto me, giving itself to me, fully and completely.

A long, low groan—hers or mine, I'm not sure. It doesn't matter. She's shaking. I'm shaking. We're coming.

I don't say it and she doesn't need to, either. Because our bodies are saying it, with every last pulse, every last tremor...

I love you.

EXTENDED EPILOGUE

Enjoy a glimpse into Bastien and Melissa's happily ever after!
Click here to start reading now.

MAILING LIST

Join the Naomi West Mailing List to receive new release alerts, free giveaways, and more!

Click the link below and you'll get sent a free motorcycle club romance as a welcome present.

JOIN NOW!
http://bit.ly/NaomiWestNewsletter

BOOKS BY NAOMI WEST

Nikolaev Bratva

Dmitry Nikolaev

Gavriil Nikolaev

Bastien Nikolaev

Sorokin Bratva

Ruined Prince

Ruined Bride

Box Sets

Devil's Outlaws: An MC Romance Box Set

Bad Boy Bikers Club: An MC Romance Box Set

The Dirty Dons Club: A Dark Mafia Romance Box Set

Dark Mafia Kingpins

Read in any order!

Andrei

Leon

Damian

Ciaran

Dirty Dons Club

Read in any order!

Sergei

Luca

Vito

Nikolai

Adrik

Bad Boy Biker's Club

Read in any order!

Dakota

Stryker

Kaeden

Ranger

Blade

Colt

Tank

Outlaw Biker Brotherhood

Read in any order!

Devil's Revenge

Devil's Ink

Devil's Heart

Devil's Vow

Devil's Sins

Devil's Scar

Other MC Standalones

Read in any order!

Maddox

Stripped

Jace

Grinder

Made in the USA
Las Vegas, NV
24 February 2023

68001539R00148